DISNEP · PIXAR

MONSTERS
UNIVERSITY

ISBN 978-0-7364-3045-6

randomhouse.com/kids

Printed in the United States of America

10 9 8 7 6 5 4 3 2 1

DISNEY · PIXAR

MONSTERS UNIVERSITY

THE JUNIOR NOVELIZATION

Adapted by Irene Trimble

Random House 🏠 New York

One sunny morning, a bright yellow school bus rolled out of an elementary school parking lot. The fall leaves were turning brilliant colors against the blue sky, and children shouted noisily from the bus. They were excited because they were going on a field trip!

The children's laughter and singing sounded typically happy, but the words to their song were a little odd: "The neck bone's connected to the head bone. The head bone's connected to the horn bone. The horn bone's right above the wing bone. . . ."

Perhaps the song *wasn't* odd for these kids. While they talked and acted like human kids, they were actually *monster* kids—and some of them did have head bones connected to their horn bones . . . as well as wing bones, extra legs, multiple eyes, tentacles, and other monster characteristics. They attended Frighton Elementary School. And today, they were visiting the famous scream factory, Monsters, Incorporated, in Monstropolis!

As the bus came to a stop in the parking lot of Monsters, Inc., Mrs. Graves, a large, kindly pink teacher with horns and glasses, stood up and faced the excited youngsters. "Okay," she said, "please remember our field trip rules: no pushing, no biting, and no fire-breathing."

The bus door flew open and little blue-horned, purple-polka-dotted, and yellow-furred monsters poured out onto the curb, laughing and shouting. One immediately breathed fire on his friend's neck.

Mrs. Graves leaned over and asked sternly, "What did I just say?" Then she tried to count the students who had come off the bus. "Eighteen, nineteen . . . ?" She glanced around at the group. "Okay, we're missing one. Who are we missing?"

She looked over at the bus, noting the closed door. A little green hand was up in the air, waving through the door window.

"Oooh, Michael!" she said, concerned.

The bus door opened, and there stood six-year-old Mike Wazowski, a round, bright green, one-eyed monster about the size of a melon. As usual, Mike was smiling.

"Thanks, Joe!" Mike called to the bus driver. "Good luck finishing your crossword puzzle!"

"Sorry, Michael," the driver replied. "I didn't

see you." It wasn't the first time the small green monster had accidentally been locked inside a bus. But Mike didn't mind. Being overlooked was something that happened to him all the time. He'd learned to make the best of it.

"That's okay," Mike answered. "When I was on the bus I found a nickel!" He jumped down from the steps and walked toward Mrs. Graves, holding up the coin and murmuring, "I wish I had pockets. . . ."

Once Mike was on the ground, Mrs. Graves couldn't help noticing just how small he was for his age. The other kids were taller and thicker, and they had lots of tentacles, eyes, and fur. Mike only had his one big eye.

Mike joined the group and Mrs. Graves did her best to corral the excited students. "Okay," she said, "everybody partner up! Get your field trip buddy!"

As the kids scrambled, Mike bounced between them, trying to find a partner. "Jeremy? You and me?" Mike anxiously asked another young monster. But Jeremy turned away. "Okay, no biggie," Mike said. He turned to another classmate. "Haley?" he asked hopefully. The other monster frowned. "No?" Mike said, watching as she headed toward another child.

"Pairing up with Claire," he said, nodding. "Great choice. She's a good egg."

Then he spotted Russell, the tallest kid in the class. "Russell!" he shouted happily. Seeing no recognition in Russell's eyes, Mike tried to jog the kid's memory. "Mike Wazowski? We carpool. We're cousins."

But Russell looked right over Mike's head, high-fived another kid, and walked off. "Okay, good catching up," Mike called after him. He looked around and saw that everyone had found a field trip buddy but him. For a second, Mike's brave smile began to falter.

Mrs. Graves walked up to him. "Well, Michael," she said, taking his hand, "it looks like it's you and me again."

Mike's smile returned, and he tugged on her hand. "Come on, Karen!" he said, eager to catch up with his classmates. "We're falling behind!"

"Please don't call me Karen," the teacher said as Mike pulled her along. Mike looked up and his eye grew wide as he and Mrs. Graves finally passed through the enormous factory doors and under the words MONSTERS, INC.

CHAPTER 2

A three-eyed tour guide met the class in the huge lobby of Monsters, Inc. Serious-looking monsters of every size and description hurried past the group. Mike was impressed. He knew they were all part of the important process of gathering screams and turning them into power for the city of Monstropolis.

"Stay close together. We're entering a very dangerous area," the guide warned. He led the students into a long, dimly lit factory room and announced, "Welcome to the scare floor!"

"Whoa!" the kids cried. Mike, at the back of the group, strained for a glimpse of the room. He was so small that he couldn't see over his classmates' shoulders.

"This is where we collect the scream energy to power our whole world," the guide explained. "Can anyone tell me whose job it is to get that scream?"

The kids yelled at the same time, "Scarers!"

"That's right!" The tour guide smiled. "Which one of you can give me the scariest roar?"

A voice came from the back of the group. "Ooh! Ooh! Sir! Right here, little green guy at two o'clock," Mike called.

The other kids shouted, too. "Me! Me!" Some even began to roar.

Mike tried harder. "Hey, guys, watch this one!" But another kid roared before Mike got a chance. And then a giant roar came from the back of the room. It was Mike! The whole group turned and stared. Mike felt pretty pleased with himself, until he realized that the class actually was staring at a group of huge Scarers approaching behind him.

The Scarers strode past the kids with cool confidence. One of them, a tall blue monster wearing a cap with the letters "MU" on it, turned to them. "Oh, hey there, kids! On tour with your school?"

"Yeah!" the kids cheered.

"Yes," Mrs. Graves said, smiling, "we're here to learn about scream energy and what it takes to be a Scarer!"

"You are?" the Scarer replied. "Well, hey, you're in luck. I just happen to be a Scarer! I learned everything I know from my school, Monsters University. Good old MU," the Scarer said. "It's the best scaring school there is."

Another Scarer, wearing a Fear Tech hat, snuck up behind the first one and snatched his MU cap. "You wish," the second one said, chuckling. "Fear Tech's the best."

The MU Scarer laughed and took his hat back. "Okay," he said to the class, "you guys tell me which school's the best." He pointed to his hat and grinned, whispering, "MU is!"

While more workers streamed onto the scare floor, the tour guide ushered the excited kids to a viewing area. As Mike studied his surroundings, he accidentally stepped over a yellow line on the floor. "Oops, stop right there," the tour guide warned him. "Don't cross that safety line." Everyone knew that human children were toxic and dangerous, so it was important to stay a safe distance away.

Mike quickly stepped back just as a row of doors was wheeled onto the floor. Again, all his classmates rushed forward, blocking his view. "Whoa, hey!" Mike protested as he was pushed and elbowed to the rear of the crowd. "Watch the eye!"

Desperate to see, Mike jumped up and down. Finally, he peeked through a sea of legs and glimpsed a door being placed into a door station. The light above the door turned red, which meant that a direct link had been created to the human world. When a Scarer stepped through this door, he'd be entering the human world through a child's closet door. Mike watched the Scarer, who was crouched and snarling. Mike figured he was warming up.

"Look, he's gonna do a real scare!" a kid in front yelled just before Mike's view was completely blocked. He tried to nudge his way forward, but one of the bigger kids pushed him back. "Out of the way, Wazowski," the kid said. "You don't belong on a scare floor." But Mike didn't believe that for a second, and he wasn't about to give up.

Mrs. Graves was trying to keep her excited students from misbehaving. "Brian," she said sharply, "do not step over the line."

Brian looked up at her and whined, "But, Mrs. Graves, Michael went over the line." Mrs. Graves looked around and was shocked to see Mike crouched behind the Scarer at the door.

"Michael!" she yelled as the Scarer opened the door to the human world and crept inside. Then, to everyone's surprise, Mike slipped into the human world right behind the Scarer!

CHAPTER

3

When Mike entered the small bedroom, his eye quickly adjusted to the darkness. He couldn't believe it. He was in the human world! His heart beating wildly, he hid in the shadows, watching as the Scarer crawled menacingly toward the sleeping boy's bed. The Scarer had no idea Mike was in there with him.

The Scarer was low, ready to spring up and scare the boy witless, when the door opened and his parents peeked in. Mike cringed—he was standing right behind the door, only inches from the humans! The Scarer quickly hid, blending in with the shadows.

"See," the boy's mom said, "I told you he's fine."

The dad shook his head. "I thought I heard something." The parents closed the door, and Mike breathed a sigh of relief. He watched the Scarer emerge from the shadows and begin to build his scare again. He scratched the bedpost, and the boy's eyes slowly opened. Then the Scarer leaped, rolled, and loomed over the bed.

Mike's jaw dropped as the boy suddenly sat up and a nerve-shattering scream filled the room.

Out on the scare floor, a scream can filled to the top. The Scarer stepped through the door and back into the safety of Monsters, Inc., smiling. He shut the door, and the class gasped.

The Scarer stopped in his tracks when he saw their panicked faces. "What?" he asked them. Then he stepped aside and saw that Mike had come through the door behind him.

Mike was smiling, and his eye had a dazed and distant look. A crowd of factory workers rushed forward. The Scarer stood back and put on his MU hat. He walked over to Mike and said sternly, "That was real dangerous, kid. I didn't even know you were in there."

Then a grin spread over the Scarer's face as he thought about what Mike had done. "Hey, I didn't even know you were in there," he repeated, impressed. "Not bad, kid." He winked at Mike. Then he placed his MU hat on Mike's head and walked away.

Mrs. Graves, however, was not impressed. "Michael! What do you have to say for yourself?"

Mike, still dazed, slowly blinked his eye. He knew now what he wanted to do for the rest of his life. "How do I become a Scarer?" he asked.

CHAPTER 4

From that day on, Mike studied like a monster possessed. He read stacks of books, learned every scare technique, memorized scare flash cards, made his own flash cards, and got the best grades he could—because he wanted to be absolutely sure he'd be accepted into Monsters University.

Years passed, and one day, the envelope he'd been waiting for arrived. He tore it open and jumped for joy. He'd done it! He'd been accepted into the Scaring Program at MU!

It wasn't long before Mike found himself on a bus again. "Monsters University!" the driver called out as the bus pulled to a stop. "Anyone getting off?"

Mike grabbed his bags and headed toward the door of the bus, beaming with pride. Before he went down the stairs, he turned to his fellow passengers. "Well, everyone, I don't mean to get emotional, but everything in my life has led me to this moment. Let it not be just the beginning of my dream, but the beginning of all our dreams." Then he addressed everyone on the bus individually. "Gladys? Promise me you'll keep auditioning! Marie, Mr. Right is out there somewhere! Phil, just keep using the ointment until that thing goes away! I wish you all the best and thank you all so much!" Then, with a "woo-hoo!", Mike bounded off the bus.

Moments later, Mike strolled through the gates of Monsters University and onto a campus of stately ivy-covered buildings. He walked to the main grassy area between buildings, called the quad, where students could meet and relax. A young monster on a skateboard whizzed by. A huge pink monster gingerly stepped over Mike as he made his way toward a stone bridge. Mike looked down and saw a class of sea monsters in an underwater section of the school. Everything was even better than he had imagined.

A monster in a "Smile Squad" T-shirt suddenly stepped up. "Hey there, freshman," he said to Mike. "I'm Jay, and I'm here to say that registration is thataway! Have a great day!"

Mike headed to the registration table, where a smiling student said, "Hey, I'm Kay. Here's your orientation packet, and you can get your picture taken with Trey!"

"Say 'Hooray!'" Trey said.

"Hooray!" Mike shouted as Trey snapped his photo. Moments later, he looked at his new student ID. The picture only showed the top of his head, but Mike didn't care. "I can't believe it!" he said, thrilled. "I'm officially a college student!" He joined a group of freshmen taking a tour of the campus.

"Okay, everyone," the student guide said. "I'm Fay, and I'll be giving you your orientation tour on this perfect day!" Mike felt like he was in a dream. Everyone was so nice. The campus was so beautiful. He stared in disbelief as Fay led the freshmen into the School of Engineering.

"This is where students learn to design and build the doors to the human world," she said, stopping at a lab. "Looks like the professor is about to test a door."

The professor activated the door, and Mike gasped as he caught a glimpse into a human child's bedroom. "And over here," Fay continued, "is the crown jewel of Monsters University: the School of Scaring." The rest of the group followed Fay, but Mike stayed behind for a moment, awed by the grandeur and history of the place.

"MU also has lots of supercool clubs and extracurriculars!" Fay said as Mike caught up with the group. They passed a row of tables offering memberships with the debate team and the painting club.

A creature who was mostly one large eye popped up behind a table and stared at Mike. "Hey there," the creature said. "Keep *your* eye in the sky at the astronomy club!" Mike quickly shook his head. He didn't think it was for him.

Turning, he saw the Greek Council table. This council oversaw the university's fraternities and sororities, social clubs whose names were based on letters of the Greek alphabet. Mike was about to pass the table by when he heard the Greek Council president say, "We sponsor the annual Scare Games."

Mike's head whipped around. "The scare what now?" he asked. The council president, a large purple-feathered creature, passed him a flyer.

"The Scare Games: a super-intense scaring competition," the vice president told Mike. "They're crazy dangerous, so *anything* could happen. And it's worth it! You get to prove you're the best."

Mike stared at the flyer, intrigued. "Cool," he said, and headed toward his dorm. He met the resident advisor, who handed him a key. "Wazowski," the RA said. "Room three-nineteen. You know, your roommate is a scare major, too."

Mike's smile lit up the hallway. Clutching the key, he rushed down the hall, murmuring, "My lifelong best friend is right behind this door!" Mike took a deep breath and pushed the door open.

A lanky lizard in purple glasses leaped from the shadows with a friendly outstretched hand. "Hey there! I'm your roomie. Name's Randy Boggs, scaring major."

Mike replied happily, "Mike Wazowski, scaring major!"

Randy smiled. "I can tell we're gonna be best chums, Mike. Take whichever bed you want. I wanted you to have first dibs!"

As Randy and Mike stood in the doorway, a student down the hall dropped a stack of boxes. Startled, Randy screamed and vanished. All Mike could see of him were his purple glasses. A second later, he reappeared.

"Sorry," Randy said worriedly. "If I do that in scaring class, I'll be a joke!"

"No," Mike told him enthusiastically, "it's totally great! You gotta use it. But lose the glasses, they give it away." Randy took off his thick purple glasses and looked around, squinting his reptilian eyes.

Mike walked into the room, chose a side, and began hanging his collection of scaring posters, along with the Scare Games flyer he'd picked up earlier. Then he checked his list. "Okay. Unpack: check. Hang posters: check. Now I need to ace my classes, graduate with honors, and become the greatest Scarer ever."

Randy shook his head. "Boy, I wish I had your confidence, Mike. Aren't you even a little nervous?"

"Actually, no. I've been waiting for this my whole life," Mike said, beaming. He pulled out the last item from his suitcase. It was the MU hat he'd gotten from the Monsters, Inc., Scarer when he was a kid. He placed it on the sill of the window that looked out onto the scaring school and smiled. "I just can't wait to get started!"

CHAPTER 5

The next day, Mike woke up bright and early. It was the first day of school! As campus bells rang out the hour, the students scurried to their classes. Mike and Randy eagerly approached the School of Scaring, went up the steps, and entered a large round classroom.

Portraits of famous scare professors hung on the walls. In front of each one was a scream can on a pedestal. Mike and Randy took their seats. Much bigger monsters sat on either side of them. One of them looked down on Mike and said, "You've gotta be kidding me."

"I'm so nervous," Randy whispered to Mike.

"Relax, it'll be fine," Mike replied as their teacher, a thick-necked, no-nonsense monster, came into the room.

"Good morning, students," he said gruffly. "Welcome to Scaring 101. My name is Professor Knight. Now, I'm sure all of you were the scariest monster in your town. Well, bad news, kids! You're in *my* town now, and I do not scare easily." He gazed around the room.

Suddenly, a shadow fell over the professor. The students gasped as he looked up to a window, where a large dark shape was perched. It flew down and landed with a *whoosh*. The class watched the monster, a tall dragon woman, flex her batlike wings and look over them with a stern frown. "Oh, Dean Hardscrabble," Professor Knight said.

Mike was thrilled as he watched Dean Hardscrabble cross the room, her centipede-like legs tapping the floor. "She's a legend," he whispered to Randy. He motioned to a container on one of the pedestals. "She broke the all-time scare record with the scream in that very can."

"I don't mean to interrupt," Dean Hardscrabble said. "I just thought I'd drop by to see the 'terrifying' faces joining my program."

"Well," the professor replied, "I'm sure my students would love to hear a few words of inspiration."

"Inspiration? Very well," she said, turning to the class. "Scariness is the true measure of a monster. If you're not scary, what kind of monster are you? It's my job to make great students greater, not mediocre students *less* mediocre."

Dean Hardscrabble gave a chilly smile. "That

is why at the end of the semester, there will be a final exam. Fail that exam, and you are out of the Scaring Program." A number of students shifted nervously. "I hope you are all properly *inspired,*" she concluded, spreading her wings and flying out through the top of the building.

Professor Knight stepped forward and quieted the murmuring class. "All right," he said, returning to the lesson. "Who can tell me the principles of an effective roar?"

A green arm shot into the air. "Yes," Professor Knight said.

Mike stood up. "There are actually five basic principles. Those include the roar's resonance, the duration of the roar, and—"

A huge, genuine *ROARRRRRN!* suddenly filled the room.

Everyone in the class turned to see where it had come from. A swaggering, eight-foot monster with blue fur and a sleepy smile stumbled into the class . . . late. "Whoops, sorry," he said. "I heard someone say 'roar,' so I just kinda went for it."

Professor Knight calmly raised an eyebrow. "Very impressive. Mr. . . . ?"

"Sullivan. Jimmy Sullivan."

The professor thought for a moment. "Hmm,

Sullivan? Like Bill Sullivan?" he asked.

"Yeah, he's my dad," the new kid replied. "You can call me Sulley."

"Hmm, I should have known you were a Sullivan. I expect big things from you," the professor said, giving Sulley a nod.

"Well, you won't be disappointed," Sulley said confidently as he took his seat.

Mike stood up again. "I'm sorry, Professor Knight, should I keep going?"

Professor Knight smiled. "No, no," he said. "Mr. Sullivan covered it." Mike sat down, disappointed. He glanced back at Sulley, who wore a smug grin.

Sulley leaned over to the student next to him. "Hey, bub. Could I borrow a pencil? I forgot all my stuff."

The student handed Sulley a pencil, which he promptly used to pick his teeth. "Yeah. There we go. That'll get it," Sulley said, dislodging a piece of something from his mouth.

Mike frowned. That Sullivan guy was so annoying!

CHAPTER 6

Mike returned to his dorm room and tacked up his school calendar, right over the Scare Games flyer he'd picked up earlier. Then he started planning his studying time for the rest of the semester.

But Randy didn't want to think about school. The first day of classes was over, so he—and most of the other kids—wanted to unwind.

"Come on, Mike. It's a fraternity and sorority party," Randy said, referring to the student Greek clubs, "We have to go!"

Mike flipped his calendar to December and marked the date for the Scaring final exam in red ink. He looked at Randy. "We flunk that scaring final, we are done. I'm not taking any chances." He sat down at his desk and pulled out a textbook.

"We've got the whole semester to study," Randy protested. "But this might be our only chance to get in good with the cool kids. That's why I made these cupcakes."

Mike looked at the tray of cupcakes Randy

held. Each one had a letter on top, and together, they spelled out BE MY dAL. Randy suddenly noticed the misspelling and twisted the cupcake with the "d" so it turned into a "p." Now the message read BE MY PAL.

"Oops," Randy said, adjusting his thick glasses. "That could have been embarrassing."

But Mike still wouldn't go. "When I'm a Scarer, life will be a nonstop party," he said, walking Randy to the door. "Stay out of trouble, wild man!"

Randy giggled. "Wild man!" He liked the sound of that.

Mike smiled, too, and closed the door. Then he rubbed his hands together, eager to dive into his books. He looked at his MU hat on the windowsill and sighed happily.

Just then, he heard a snuffling noise and a strange pig-faced animal popped up at his window. "What the . . . ?" Mike said in confusion.

The creature snorted as it flopped through the window and landed on the floor, its six legs flailing. Mike jumped back when it ran around the floor wildly. Then a large blue hand appeared on the windowsill.

"ARCHIE!" Sulley yelled as he fell into Mike's room with a thud. The pig ran over

Sulley's stomach and under Mike's bed.

"Hey!" Mike shouted, jumping onto a chair. "What are you doing?"

"Shhhh," Sulley replied. "Shhhh."

"Wait," Mike said. "You're shushing me? You can't shush m—" But before he could finish, Sulley put his big blue hand over Mike's mouth.

Sulley peeked out the window and saw four big Fear Tech guys run by. "Where'd he go?" one called out. "That guy's in big trouble!" They were scouring the campus for Sulley.

"Hey, guys, over here!" another shouted, and they all took off.

Sulley watched them leave. "Fear Tech dummies," he said, chuckling. Mike mumbled something, and Sulley realized he still had his hand clamped over Mike's mouth. "Oh, sorry about that, buddy," he said, and let Mike go.

Mike was gasping for air. "Why are you in my room?" he asked angrily.

Sulley seemed confused for a second. "*Your* room?" He looked around and said, "Huh, this is not my room," then shrugged and turned his attention back to the pig. "Archie? Come here, boy!"

"Archie?" Mike asked in disbelief.

"Archie the Scare Pig," Sulley said as he

kneeled down and tried to pull the animal from under the bed. "He's Fear Tech's mascot. I stole it! Gonna take it to the RORs."

"The what?" Mike asked.

Sulley stood up. "Roar Omega Roar? The top fraternity on campus? They only accept the 'highly elite,'" he said, poking his big blue chest with his thumb. Then he turned back to the creature. "Okay," he told Mike, "I'll lift the bed, you grab the pig. Ready?"

"What? No, no!" Mike cried as Sulley quickly counted to three and then shoved Mike under the bed. The bed bumped and bucked as Mike struggled underneath.

"Don't let go!" Sulley called out. "And watch out. He's a biter!" Archie shot out from under the bed, dragging Mike behind him. He ran over Sulley, leaped out of Mike's hands, and landed on top of Mike's bookcase.

Sulley quickly began climbing after him. He reached for the creature, shouting, "I got 'im!" just as the whole bookcase came crashing to the floor.

Sulley landed on the floor, laughing. "That was awesome!" Then he looked at Mike. "What am I doing? I haven't introduced myself: James P. Sullivan."

"Mike Wazowski," Mike said, trying to lead Sulley toward the door. "Listen, it was quite delightful meeting you and whatever that is, but if you don't mind, I have to study my scaring."

Sulley rolled his eyes. "Pssh, you don't need to study scaring, you just do it."

"Really?" Mike replied. "I think there's a little more to it than that. But hey, thanks for stopping by." Mike was about to open the door when he turned and saw the pig . . . with his beloved MU hat in its mouth. "Let go of that!" Mike shouted, and lunged for the hat. But Archie leaped out the window. "My hat!" Mike screamed as he dashed through the doorway, hoping to intercept the pig outside.

"My pig!" Sulley shouted, following right behind him.

Mike desperately chased the pig as it bolted through campus. When he finally got close enough, he made a flying leap onto Archie's back and grabbed the Fear Tech blanket that was strapped around the critter's body.

"Yeah!" Sulley cheered, watching Mike bounce up and down on Archie's back. "Ride it to Frat Row!"

Mike winced as Archie barely missed a guitar-playing student, who was crooning a ballad to several girls. Then Sulley crashed through the little group and sent them all sprawling. Laughing, he raced after Archie and Mike, who were heading toward the party lights of Frat Row.

Still at top speed, Mike rode Archie through several fraternity parties of dancing monsters. Sulley grabbed a piece of pizza off a Ping-Pong table in one house as he passed by. "Yeah!" he cheered again as they all raced out the back door.

Mike suddenly saw his roommate, Randy. "Cupcake?" Randy asked. Mike couldn't stop

Archie from smashing into Randy. His cupcakes sailed into the air and splatted down on his head, one by one, spelling out LAME.

Mike and Archie veered around a corner and made a direct hit into a husky monster playing football outside. The impact left Mike gasping on the ground while Archie continued running. Sulley leaped over Mike, chasing the scare pig.

But Archie still had Mike's hat. Desperate, Mike looked around and noticed a trash can at the end of a row of bikes. Archie was running right by them.

Mike stood up, grabbed the husky monster's football, and timed his throw perfectly. It hit the first bike and the rest fell like dominoes, knocking the trash can right into Archie's path. Unable to stop himself, Archie ran into the can. Mike dashed over, picked up the squealing creature, and grabbed his MU hat. "Ha-ha!" he yelled triumphantly.

Just then, Sulley grabbed them both and hoisted them into the air like a trophy. "Fear Tech's mascot! MU rules!" he shouted to the partying students.

As the crowd cheered, someone slapped an MU sticker over Archie's Fear Tech blanket. Mike was beginning to feel like a hero as the crowd chanted, "MU! MU! MU!"

Several fraternity brothers headed toward him. "Did you see him catch that pig? You are Jaws Theta Chi material, freshman!"

Mike was so flattered. "Well, thanks, I didn't know the—" he started to say, but the fraternity boys walked right past him and over to Sulley.

"No, no," another fraternity boy said, patting Sulley on the back. "He's an Omega Howl guy."

Mike was feeling pretty annoyed, when a voice suddenly called out, "I'll take it from here, gentlemen!" Everyone turned to see a huge monster with large horns and terrifying fangs step forward from the crowd. He wore a jacket with the letters "ROR" on it.

The horned monster lumbered up to Sulley. "Johnny Worthington," he said, introducing himself, "president of Roar Omega Roar. What's your name, Big Blue?"

"Jimmy Sullivan. Friends call me Sulley."

"Whoa! This guy's a Sullivan!" exclaimed Chet, another ROR member.

"Chet, calm down," Johnny said. Then he turned to Sulley. "Any freshman with the guts to pull off a stunt like that has got 'Future Scarer' written all over him."

Sulley nodded smugly. Johnny and the RORs

quickly swept Sulley into their fraternity house while Mike trailed along behind. "Did you see me ride the pig? That took guts!" he called after them.

Chet turned and stopped Mike at the door. "Slow down, squirt. This party's for scare students only."

Johnny leaned down to Mike's level. "Sorry, killer, but you might want to hang out with someone a little more your speed. You know, like those guys." Johnny pointed to a presentation that another fraternity had set up nearby. A group of awkward-looking monsters surrounded a table, which was decorated with kiddie balloons and cake. The sign said OOZMA KAPPA.

Mike looked at them, horrified. One of them yelled, "Oh, hey dere! Wanna join Oozma Kappa? We have cake!"

Mike stared at Johnny in disbelief. "Is that a joke?" he asked.

Johnny sighed with annoyance. "Sulley, talk to your friend," he said.

"Well," Sulley replied, "he's not really my friend, but sure." He turned to Mike. "You heard him; this is a party for scare students."

Mike was exasperated. "I *am* a scare student!"

Sulley shrugged. "I mean, for scare students who actually, you know, have a chance." The remark cut Mike to the core. His eye narrowed angrily as the RORs laughed.

"My chances are as good as yours!" Mike fired back. "You just wait, hotshot! I'm gonna scare circles around you this year."

"Okay," Sulley said, laughing as he headed into the ROR house with his new friends. "I'd like to see that."

"Oh, don't worry," Mike said as he put on his MU hat and walked away. "You will."

Mike dedicated himself to his studies with more determination than ever. He listened intently as Professor Knight broke down the science of scaring. "Ready position," the professor said as the students took their stances. "Common Crouch," he instructed them. "I want to see matted fur and yellowed teeth! Show me some slobber! Drool is a tool! Use it!" Mike growled and slobbered for all he was worth.

The professor walked around the room, making adjustments in the students' poses. When he got to Sulley, he stopped. "Now, here is a monster who looks like a Scarer!" he said. Mike glared at Sulley, who was grinning.

"If you want a hope of passing this class, you better eat, breathe, and sleep scaring," the professor warned the students.

Mike took the teacher's advice to heart. He read piles of books, memorizing different scare techniques. He practiced for hours, roaring in the mirror.

Sulley used his textbooks, too—but not quite

the same way. He used them to steady a Ping-Pong table at the ROR fraternity house.

Days passed and Mike never quit. Fall football arrived on campus, but Mike paid no attention. Instead, he spent hours in his room while Randy quizzed him.

"Fear of spiders?" Randy asked.

"Arachnophobia," Mike answered quickly.

"Fear of thunder?"

"Keraunophobia," Mike replied.

"Fear of chopsticks?"

"Consecotaleophobia," Mike said. He looked up impatiently. "What is this, kindergarten? Give me a hard one."

The semester continued, and Mike's efforts began to pay off. For a quiz, Professor Knight listed multiple-choice answers on the chalkboard. Mike's hand shot up first. "The answer is C, 'Fangs.'"

"Well done, Mr. Wazowski," Professor Knight said.

"A clown running in the dark!" Mike confidently answered the professor's next question.

"Right again!" Professor Knight told him.

"Warts, boils, and moles, in that order," Mike said, totally dominating the test.

"Outstanding!" Professor Knight said, impressed. Sulley looked over to Mike and gave him a nasty look. But Mike didn't care. He knew he'd get the last laugh. It was October, and the semester was half over. The midterm exam was the next day.

=M=

After the exam, Sulley walked down the steps of the School of Scaring, holding his test results. He grinned and gave Johnny a thumbs-up. He'd passed. Johnny put an arm around him. Then Mike came dashing down the stairs, happily waving his A-plus score.

Sulley unfolded his exam to reveal a lowly C-minus. Johnny and the RORs exchanged a worried look. And for the first time, Sulley wasn't feeling that warm, ROR brotherly love.

Mike, however, was fired up. He couldn't wait to take the final exam. Even when he was working at his student job, he studied. Every day, he punched in his work-study card and then steered a floor polisher with one hand while holding a book on scare tactics with the other. He was so focused that he paid no attention to his surroundings. Other students had to jump out of his way as he tore past.

In the classroom, Mike showed his technique to Professor Knight. He expertly displayed all the important poses: Pirhana-Jaw, Ogre's Slump, even the Zombie Snarl. "That's some remarkable improvement, Michael," Professor Knight said.

When it was his turn, Sulley stood, made a scary face, and let out an incredible roar. But Professor Knight shook his head and said, "One frightening face does not a Scarer make, Mr. Sullivan." Sulley sat back down, his confidence fraying.

Afterward, Mike went back to his dorm room and ripped another page off his calendar. The day for the final exams was circled in red. This was it. December had finally arrived!

CHAPTER 9

On the big day, Mike and Randy were nervous but determined. They quizzed each other as they headed toward the School of Scaring.

From the ROR house across campus, Sulley saw Mike and scowled. "I am going to wipe the floor with that little know-it-all," Sulley told his ROR brothers.

"Yes, yes, you are, Big Blue." Then, to Sulley's shock, Johnny removed Sulley's ROR jacket and hung it over his own arm.

"Hey! Wait. What are you—"

Johnny smiled. "It's just a precaution. RORs are the best Scarers on campus, Sullivan. Can't have a member come in second to a beach ball."

"I'm gonna destroy that guy!" Sulley protested.

Johnny held up the jacket. "Well, then you'll get this back in no time. It's time to start delivering on that Sullivan name."

Sulley entered the classroom and dropped into a seat next to Mike and Randy. Professor Knight addressed the students. "Today's final will judge your ability to assess a child's fear and perform the appropriate scare . . . in the scare simulator." Turning, he motioned toward a modular room that looked like a human child's bedroom. A small robotic child was tucked into the bed. The students stared at the machine nervously.

"Dean Hardscrabble is with us this morning to see who will be moving on in the Scaring Program and who will not," Professor Knight continued. He gestured to Dean Hardscrabble, who stood to the side, unsmiling, as she casually adjusted her record-breaking scream can. "Let's get started!"

Soon, the first student stood onstage, ready to begin. "I am a five-year-old girl afraid of spiders and Santa Claus," Professor Knight said. "Which scare do you use?"

The student gulped as Dean Hardscrabble stretched her bat wings and flew up to a window. "Uh, that's a Seasonal Creep-and-Crawl," the student said.

"Demonstrate," Professor Knight said.

The student walked through the door of the simulator, then lunged, roaring at the robotic child in bed. The student looked at Professor Knight, hoping he'd done it correctly. But the professor simply said, "Results will be posted outside my office. Next!"

As students waited their turn at the simulator, Mike took out his textbook for some last-minute cramming. Feeling resentful, Sulley stared at his rival. Then he noticed that the RORs were in the gallery, watching. Johnny gave Sulley a nod. Sulley nodded back, but he wasn't feeling it.

Sulley stood up and walked past Mike, "accidentally" knocking his books to the floor. "Hey, do you mind?" Mike said.

Sulley shrugged. "Don't mind at all," he said, and began to stretch, warming up for his turn at the simulator.

Randy looked over at Sulley and said, "Come on, Mike. Let's just move."

Mike nodded and began to walk away. Then he changed his mind. He walked back to Sulley. "Stay out of my way," he said. "I worked really hard for this, unlike you."

Sulley just grinned and said, "That's because you don't belong here."

Mike stood there for a moment, his anger building. Then he turned to Sulley—and let out a loud *ROAR!*

Sulley flinched. Then he glanced into the stands and saw his ROR fraternity brothers watching. He couldn't let them think he was backing down. He took a deep breath and responded: *"ROARRRR!"* This time it was Mike's turn to flinch. Sulley laughed. "That's what I thought," he said under his breath.

Sulley went back to practicing, but Mike wasn't willing to let it go. He got in Sulley's face and roared again. It wasn't long before the class's attention was turned to the two monsters facing off against each other.

"ROARR!"

"ROARRR!"

"ROOAARRRR!"

Randy looked up and saw that Dean Hardscrabble was watching, too. Sulley and Mike were moving closer to each other, roaring louder and louder. Then Sulley took a step back and accidentally bumped into the pedestal holding Dean Hardscrabble's famous scream can.

Everyone watched in horror as the scream can wobbled and clanged to the floor!

Mike and Sulley froze as the can rolled across the room. It came to a stop, apparently undamaged. Both monsters let out a sigh of relief.

But just then, the can burst open—and a horrifying scream escaped! Students gasped and ran for cover as the can spun wildly around the room like a deflating balloon while the ear-splitting scream escaped. At last, it fell in front of Mike and Sulley with a gurgle. The scream can was completely empty.

A huge dark figure, wings outstretched, landed in front of Mike and Sulley. They were face to face with Dean Hardscrabble. She picked up her drained can. Randy immediately disappeared.

"I'm so sorry," Mike said.

"It was an accident," Sulley added.

Dean Hardscrabble shrugged and looked into the empty, twisted can. "What, this?" Her tone was unnervingly steady. "My one souvenir from a lifetime of scaring? Well, accidents happen, don't they? The important thing is no one got hurt."

Mike and Sulley were stunned. "You're taking this remarkably well," Mike said gratefully.

Dean Hardscrabble nodded. "Now, let's continue the exams," she said, looking at Mike. "Mr. Wazowski, I'm a five-year-old girl on a farm in Kansas afraid of lightning. Which scare do you use?"

Mike looked around, confused. "Shouldn't I go up on the simulator?" he asked.

Dean Hardscrabble leaned toward him. "Which scare do you use?" she repeated sternly.

Mike quickly gathered his wits and answered, "That is a Shadow Approach with a Cackle Holler."

"Demonstrate," Dean Hardscrabble said.

Mike took a deep breath. This was it. It was all on the line. But before he could even begin, Dean Hardscrabble spoke again: "Stop! Thank you."

"But I didn't get to—" Mike started to say.

"I've seen enough," Dean Hardscrabble said, and turned away. She looked at Sulley to indicate it was his turn. "I'm a seven-year-old boy—"

Before she could complete her sentence,

Sulley stepped up and let out a ferocious *ROARRR!*

Dean Hardscrabble's dragon eyes narrowed. "I wasn't finished," she snapped.

"I don't need any of that stuff to scare," Sulley replied confidently.

"That 'stuff,'" Dean Hardscrabble said, "would have informed you that this particular child is afraid of snakes. So a roar wouldn't make him scream. It would make him cry, alerting his parents, exposing the monster world, destroying life as we know it, and of course we can't have that. So I'm afraid I cannot recommend that you continue in the Scaring Program. Good day."

Sulley laughed, unable to believe she could possibly mean it. Then he saw the cold look in her eyes. "Wait, what? But I'm a Sullivan!"

Dean Hardscrabble smiled. "Well, then I'm sure your family will be very disappointed."

Sulley looked around the room, confused. He was sure someone was going to say it was all a big mistake. But then he spotted Johnny and his ROR brothers as they left the gallery, taking his fraternity jacket with them.

As Sulley stumbled away in shock, Dean Hardscrabble turned back to Mike. "And, Mr.

Wazowski, I'm afraid what you lack is something that cannot be taught. You're not scary. You will not be continuing in the Scaring Program."

It hit Mike like a freight train. "No, you've made a mistake," he said. "Please, let me try the simulator. I'll surprise you!"

"I doubt that very much," Dean Hardscrabble replied. She nodded to Professor Knight, who motioned the next student forward.

Mike was dumbstruck. Just like that, it was over. He left the class feeling like someone had sucked all the oxygen out of his world.

CHAPTER

11

Weeks passed, and soon it was January and the start of a new semester. Back in class, Mike fidgeted in his seat as Professor Brandywine lectured about scream-can designs. This was Mike's new major. He stared out the window at the School of Scaring in the distance and wondered how it had all gone so wrong.

"Some say a career as a Scream Can Designer is boring, unchallenging, a waste of a monster's potential. . . ." Professor Brandywine droned on in a toneless voice. Mike couldn't have agreed more.

Across the classroom, Sulley sat and glared at Mike. In Sulley's mind, things at MU had been perfect until Mike Wazowski ruined it all.

When the class finally ended, Mike dejectedly headed back to his dorm. Sulley, still glaring furiously, followed Mike across most of the campus. He was seething, and he wanted Mike to know it.

But Mike paid no attention to Sulley. He was too sad. He went straight to his dorm room and stared at his MU hat. He was heartbroken. He picked up his scream-can design textbook and sighed. Then he hurled it against the wall. As the book hit, it knocked down his calendar . . . revealing the Greek Scare Games flyer Mike had tacked to the wall on the first day of school.

Mike moved closer, staring at the flyer. Slowly, a smile grew across his face. He tore the paper off the wall and ran to the door. Opening it, he found Sulley standing there, still glaring. "Out of my way!" Mike shouted, and rushed down the hall.

Mike tore out of the building and ran toward Fraternity Row. A crowd of fraternity and sorority monsters filled the area, facing a large outdoor stage.

— M —

Mike watched the Greek Council president stand up and address the crowd. "Welcome to this year's Greek Scare Games kickoff!" she said. Everyone cheered, yelling support for the fraternities and sororities that were competing. Then the council president continued. "We have a special guest. The founder of the Games, Dean Hardscrabble!"

The crowd cheered once again as Dean

Hardscrabble stepped to the podium. "Good afternoon," she said in a low growl. "As a student, I created these games as a friendly competition. But be prepared: to take home the trophy, you must be the most fearsome monsters on campus!" After another round of cheers, she ended with a faint smile. "Good luck, and may the best monsters win!"

The president smiled and announced, "All right, everybody! Sign-ups for the Scare Games are officially—"

But before she could say "closed," Mike shouted from the crowd, "WAIT! I'm signing up!"

Dean Hardscrabble's eyes narrowed as Mike pushed through the crowd. "You have to be in a fraternity to compete," the council president reminded Mike.

Mike turned and desperately scanned the crowd. Finally, he pointed to the only fraternity he thought might let him join. "Behold! The next winning fraternity of the Scare Games," he said grandly, "*the* brothers, *my* brothers, of Oozma Kappa!"

The crowd turned to see the Oozma Kappa members, who looked almost as shocked as everyone else. The oddball group stood proudly, though: a balding, middle-aged monster; a scrawny two-headed, four-armed monster; a rosy-cheeked blob with a multitude of eyes; and a shy, shaggy-haired monster. "Hi," the blobby kid said awkwardly. The balloon he was holding suddenly deflated, and the crowd howled with laughter.

Dean Hardscrabble approached Mike. "Mr. Wazowski," she said sternly, "what are you doing?"

"You just said the winners are the most fearsome monsters on campus," Mike replied. "If I win, it means you kicked out the best Scarer in the whole school."

"That won't happen," Dean Hardscrabble said flatly.

"Then how about a little wager?" Mike said. A murmur of shock rose from the crowd. Was a student actually challenging her to a bet? Dean Hardscrabble shot him a predatory look. For a moment, Mike felt like she was going to splash soy sauce on him and eat him like an egg roll. But he stood his ground. "If I win, you let me back in the Scaring Program."

"And what would that prove?" she snarled.

Mike replied, "That you were wrong."

Dean Hardscrabble thought for a moment as

she reappraised the little green monster standing in front of her. "Very well," she said finally. "If you win, I will let your entire team into the Scaring Program. But if you lose, you will pack up your things and leave Monsters University."

"Deal," Mike said.

"Now all you need to do is find enough members to compete," Dean Hardscrabble said.

Mike looked at his little group and didn't see that he had a problem. He turned to the Greek Council president and asked, "What? We need six guys, right?"

"We count bodies, not heads," the president said, pointing to the two-headed monster. "That dude counts as one."

Dean Hardscrabble smiled as she watched Mike's panicked reaction. "Anyone else want to join our team?" Mike asked the crowd. "Anyone at all?"

Suddenly, Mike spotted his roommate in the crowd. "Randy! Randy, thank goodness, I need you on my team!"

"Oh, sorry, Mike," Randy said. "I'm already on a team." Randy walked over to Johnny, and Mike saw that he was wearing a ROR jacket.

"Boggs!" Johnny turned to Randy with a chuckle. "Do the trick!" With a pained smile,

Randy made himself disappear. The RORs burst out laughing.

Mike was desperate. He jumped on top of a nearby parked car and shouted, "Please, anybody! I need one more monster. Just one more!"

But no one answered.

Mike stared into the crowd, hoping someone—anyone—might want to join Oozma Kappa. Finally, the Greek Council president looked at Mike and said, "Yeah, sorry, doesn't look good. We have to move on. Your team doesn't qualify."

Suddenly, a voice rang out, "Yes, it does!" A large figure stepped through the crowd and climbed on top of the car with Mike. It was Sulley, who had followed Mike and watched the whole display. "The star player has just arrived," he said.

"You?" Mike said, staring at Sulley. "No way!" He turned back to the crowd. "Someone else, please! *Anyone* else!"

The Greek Council president was losing patience. "We're shutting down the sign-ups," she said. "Is he on your team or not?"

Mike threw his little green arms up in surrender and yelled, "*Gaah!* Fine, yes. He's on my team."

Dean Hardscrabble smiled coldly at Mike.

"Good luck," she said, and walked off.

Sulley just shrugged. "All right, Wazowski, what's the plan?"

— ᴍ —

That evening, Mike and Sulley headed over to the Oozma Kappa house, carrying their suitcases. Soon, they reached a prim little house with a covered porch and lace curtains hanging in the windows. "This is a frat house?" Sulley asked.

A balding middle-aged monster opened the door and greeted them warmly. "Hey there, team-mateys!" he said, waving a tentacle. "Come on aboard! It is my honor to welcome you to your new home!"

Mike and Sulley exchanged a dubious look as the fellow ushered them into a house that looked like it belonged to somebody's grandmother. The place was filled with knickknacks and needlepoint pillows. "We call this room 'Party Central,'" a little blobby monster said with a grin.

"Technically, we haven't had a party here yet," one part of the two-headed monster explained.

"But when we do," the other head added,

"we'll be ready!" He flipped a switch on a remote, and a disco ball dropped from the ceiling—and crashed to the floor.

The older monster handed Mike a mug. "Whoo! Hot-cocoa train is coming through. Whoa . . . next stop . . . you!"

Mike tried to get things back on track by addressing his team firmly. "I would like to start us off first by—"

But Sulley interrupted. "So . . . ," he said, eyeing the Oozma Kappa crew skeptically, "you guys are in the Scaring Program?"

"We wish!" the balding monster replied. "None of us lasted very long. Guess we just weren't what old Hardscrabble was looking for." He handed Sulley his business card. "Don Carlton, 'mature' student," he said with a sigh. "Thirty years in the textile industry and then ol' dandy Don got downsized. Figured I could throw myself a pity party or go back to school and learn the computers."

Mike and Sulley nodded blankly, then turned to the yellow two-headed monster. "Hi, I'm Terry with a 'Y'!" one of the heads said.

"And I'm Terri with an 'I'!" the shorter but almost-identical head said. "My brother may have gotten the height, but I got—"

"The good looks!" they exclaimed at the same time. The two heads turned to each other and smiled.

Then a big burly monster who was mostly two huge legs and purple fur gruffly introduced himself. "Hey! I'm Art. New Age philosophy major. Excited to live with you and laugh with you . . . and cry with you," he finished emotionally, wiping his eyes. He handed Mike and Sulley each a journal with a unicorn on the cover. Sulley looked at it like it was diseased. "I thought you might like to keep a dream journal," Art explained.

Suddenly, the little blobby monster popped up behind Sulley. Sulley jumped and yelled.

"My name's Scott Squibbles," the blob said, blinking his five eyes. "My friends call me Squishy. I'm undeclared, unattached, and pretty much unwelcome anywhere but here."

Mike tried to take control of the group again. "Well, now that we've been introduced, as captain of our team—" he began, but Sulley interrupted once more.

"So basically, you guys have no scaring experience?" Sulley asked.

All the Oozma Kappas began to laugh. "Not a lot!" Squishy said. "But now we've got you!"

Don nodded enthusiastically. "You're about the scariest feller I've ever seen, even with them pink polka-dots."

Mike looked at them all in disbelief. "Well, actually," he said, "I think *I* bring the whole package." But no one seemed to be listening. Squishy had already taken Sulley's huge hand and was holding it up to his head.

"Your hand is bigger than my whole face!" Squishy said, starstruck.

"He's like a mountain with fur!" Terri added.

"We thought our dreams were over, but Mike said if we win, they're letting us in the Scaring Program!" Don called out.

"We're gonna be real Scarers!" Terry yelled excitedly.

"Yeah, right," Sulley said doubtfully. He shot Mike a nervous, suspicious look. But Mike just smiled and nodded, as if anything was possible.

Later that night, Don led Mike and Sulley to their room. "And here's what you've been waitin' for, fellas—your very own Oozma Kappa bedroom!" he said, switching on the light. Mike and Sulley looked around the tiny room with bunk beds. Don smiled. "We'll let you guys get settled," he said cheerfully. "Anything you need, you just give a big holler-oony!"

Sulley nodded as Don closed the door and left. Then he turned to Mike. "Are you kidding me?" he asked, convinced the Oozmas could never become Scarers.

"Look, they don't have to be good. I'm going to carry the whole team," Mike replied.

"Really? And who's going to carry you?" Sulley huffed.

Mike was suddenly furious. "Hey, you want to go back to Can Design, you know where the door is!"

Sulley shuffled his big feet. Mike was right. They were going to have to make good here. Just then, the lights went out. Sulley flicked the light switch. Nothing happened. "Great," Sulley muttered.

"Guys? Anybody home?" Mike said as he and Sulley felt their way through the darkened house. A door creaked open, revealing stairs to the basement. "Um, hello?" Mike said, seeing a dim light. "Fellas?"

Mike and Sulley stepped down into the basement. A single candle flickered in the center of the room. They flinched as a robed monster stepped forward from the shadows. "Do you pledge your souls to the Oozma Kappa brotherhood?" the robed figure asked solemnly. The figure's hood fell back a little, revealing a mustache. It was Don.

Someone suddenly whacked Mike on the behind with a paddle. "OW!" Mike yelled.

A robed two-headed monster stepped from behind them. One head said, "Do you swear to keep secret," and the second head finished, "all that you learn here?"

Sulley was whacked on the behind, too. "HEY!" he shouted angrily.

Squishy emerged from the shadows dressed in a black robe. "Will you take the oath of the—" he began, when the lights came on brightly. A roly-poly monster in pink hair curlers waddled down the stairs, carrying a basket of laundry.

"Oh, for cryin' out loud, Mom!" Squishy said, squinting at the light. "We're doing an initiation!"

"Oooh, scary!" Ms. Squibbles said. "Well, carry on. Just pretend I'm not here."

Squishy looked at Mike and Sulley, embarrassed. "This is my mom's house," he explained as Ms. Squibbles loaded the washer. Squishy sighed and started again. "Do you promise to look out for your brothers, no matter what the peril?"

As Squishy recited the oath, Ms. Squibbles put a pair of sneakers in the dryer and turned it on. Squishy tried to talk over the sound of the sneakers thudding louder and louder. "Will you defend Oozma Kappa, no matter how dangerous? In the face of unending pain?" Squishy yelled over the constant *th-thud, th-thud* of the sneakers in the dryer. "Sacrificing all that you—" *Th-thud.* "Oh, forget it," Squishy said, finally giving up. "You're in."

The brothers of Oozma Kappa crowded around Mike and Sulley. "Look, we know we're no one's first choice for a fraternity," Don said. "So it means a lot to have you here with us."

"I can't wait to start scaring with you

brothers," Squishy told Mike and Sulley, hugging them awkwardly. He handed them each an Oozma Kappa baseball hat. Mike put his on. Then he looked at Sulley, who stood with the cap in his hand as if he hadn't quite made up his mind. Finally, Sulley put the tiny cap on his giant head, and the Oozmas cheered.

Terri and Terry rushed over to Sulley and whacked him on the behind again. Sulley turned, grabbed the paddle, and snapped it in half.

"*Ahh!*" Terri and Terry screamed as they scurried away.

The group happily headed upstairs to the living room. "Time for a celebration!" Squishy said. "Grab the couch cushions, gentlemen, 'cause we're building a fort!"

The next morning, Mike rolled over in his bunk and onto a pillow of blue fur. Still snoring, Mike cuddled up to it and murmured, "I know you're a princess and I'm just a stable boy. . . ." Then he opened his eye and saw he was embracing Sulley's hand, which was hanging down from the upper bunk. *"AGHHHH!"* Mike screamed as he pushed the hand away.

Sulley woke up with a start and toppled out of bed. "What are you doing?" he yelled at Mike.

"Your grubby paw was in my bed!" Mike yelled back.

Sulley's eyes narrowed. "Were you kissing my hand?"

Mike pretended to laugh. "Kissing your hand? No! And what about all your shedding?"

"I don't shed," Sulley replied.

"Really?" Mike asked skeptically. He pounded Sulley's mattress, and a cloud of blue hair rose into the air.

Sulley just grumbled and tried to maneuver around Mike.

"Excuse me," said Mike, who was heading for the door. "Would you just let me—"

"I just want to get my stuff," Sulley growled.

The two started to struggle as they tried to move around the little room, until both of them tumbled out the bedroom door and onto the hallway floor.

Suddenly, there was a flash! Mike and Sulley looked up to see all the Oozmas gathered in the hallway. "First morning in the house!" Squishy exclaimed, holding up a camera.

"That's going in the album!" Art added.

Don came running up the stairs. "Guys! We got a letter! It's the first event of the Scare Games!" Mike, Sulley, and the other OKs quickly gathered around. Mike tried to take the letter from Don, but it kept sticking to the older monster's tentacles. Don smiled meekly and struggled with the letter, muttering an apology, "Tentacles . . . sticky."

Finally, Mike tore it loose and read the details. "Wait a second," Mike said, surprised. "They want us to meet *where*?"

=**M**=

That night, Mike, Sulley, and the Oozmas stepped into the campus's large, dark sewer drain. Water dripped from the ceiling, and the sound of their footsteps echoed eerily in the cold, damp tunnel. They turned a corner and saw a crowd. The Greek Council president and her vice president stood on a stage in the center of the floodlit sewer.

"Welcome to the first competition of the Scare Games: the Toxicity Challenge!" the president said to the competing sororities and fraternities. "Every Scarer that enters a child's room has to navigate a minefield of deadly toxicity, because there is nothing more toxic than a human child!"

The vice president continued, "But thanks to MU's biology department, we've found a close second—the stinging glow urchin!"

The Oozmas watched a group of students carry in a large wooden box. The president reached inside with a metal claw and pulled out a round, spiky blue creature that hissed and sparked menacingly.

"Oooh," Art said softly. "I want to touch it."

The president pointed to the side of the stage, toward a tunnel strewn with hundreds of the glowing, crackling urchins. Art seemed even more intrigued. "This is the starting line," the vice president said. "The light at the end of the tunnel is the finish line. Whoever comes in

Mike Wazowski has always wanted to
be a Scarer at Monsters, Inc.

Mike is accepted into the School of
Scaring at Monsters University!

Mike decorates his dorm room with school posters. The Scare Games include some of the craziest events on campus.

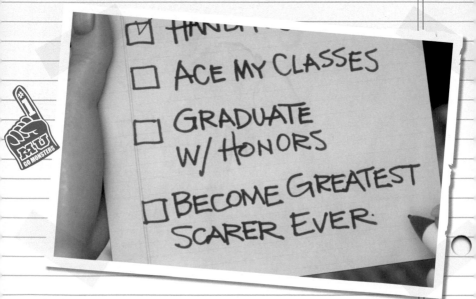

☑ HANDA...
☐ ACE MY CLASSES
☐ GRADUATE W/ HONORS
☐ BECOME GREATEST SCARER EVER.

From his very first day at college, Mike knows exactly what he wants to do.

James "Sulley" Sullivan thinks he can
cruise through the Scaring Program
without studying.

Mike and Sulley join the Oozma Kappa
fraternity so they can enter the
Scare Games.

I ♥ MU

Don Carlton welcomes new members Mike
and Sulley to the Oozma Kappa house.

Squishy is happy to have new
friends in Oozma Kappa.

The Oozma Kappas try to make their
initiation ceremony spooky, but someone
turns on the lights.

Deep down, Sulley worries that the Oozma
Kappas are just not very scary.

For inspiration, Mike takes the team to
one of the most famous scare locations
ever: Monsters, Inc.!

SCARERS

Mike and his friends peek through a
window and watch monsters at work on
a scare floor.

Monsters can look different and be
scary in different ways. Mike thinks
that's an important lesson.

Security guards spot the Oozma Kappas at
Monsters, Inc. The Oozma Kappas run and have
the best night of their lives.

Sulley gives Mike some scaring tips on the night before the final Scare Games event.

Mike believes he has what it takes to scare children in the human world.

last is eliminated from the Games."

"Eliminated?" Terry gasped.

Mike looked him in the eye. "We're not going to lose; all we need is right here," he said, pointing to his chest.

Squishy smiled. "You mean heart?"

"No, I mean me," Mike replied. "I'm gonna win the race for us."

Sulley looked at Mike like he'd lost his mind. "All right," Sulley said, pushing Mike out of the way. "That's very cute, but move, move. *I'm* gonna win this."

Mike pushed Sulley right back. "It's an obstacle course!" he said, looking up at him. "What are you going to do? Roar at it?"

The PNK sorority, in their bright pink tees, gathered next to the Oozmas. "Okay," one of the PNKs said to her team. "This is all about teamwork, so let's stick together!"

As the teams came to the starting line, the Greek Council president made a final announcement. "Attention, teams, one last thing. Scarers work in the *dark*."

Suddenly, the floodlit sewer went black. And the Oozma Kappas went from nervous to completely terrified.

CHAPTER

15

In the darkness, the toxic urchins glowed and sparked ominously. "I want to go home!" Squishy cried.

"On your marks!" the Greek Council vice president said. "Get set!"

Mike glared at Sulley, and Sulley glared right back as all the teams shifted in place, ready to race. The rest of the Oozmas were behind them, but Mike and Sulley didn't even notice. This was a grudge match between the two of them.

"GO!" the vice president yelled.

"AHHHH!" Art shouted, charging into the tunnel first. Surprised, the Oozmas and the other teams followed. Art immediately hit a glow urchin and screamed as it sparked and shocked him over and over. "Whoa!" Art yelled. His leg began to swell from the stings.

Then Squishy howled as the urchins stung him, and he stumbled. The PNKs leaped over the falling Oozmas and moved up behind Mike and Sulley.

Mike and Sulley were running neck and neck,

carefully navigating the stinging urchins. "That as fast as you can go?" Mike yelled at Sulley.

"Just getting started!" Sulley yelled back as they entered the portion of the dark tunnel with hanging blue urchins.

"Uh, guys!" Don called out from the rear. "We're falling behind a little. FELLAS?"

A swinging urchin hit Sulley's arm, and Mike gained the lead. But Sulley put his head down and ran forward, taking hit after hit. He caught up to Mike and ran past him. He could see the ROR team ahead.

Just when Sulley reached his former brothers, he stumbled and fell. The RORs left him in the dust. "Later, loser," Chet said as Sulley got up with a growl.

Mike suddenly ran past Sulley, but Sulley wasn't about to give up. He barreled through the urchins, taking shock after shock. But it was the RORs who came out of the tunnel first. The crowd cheered as the council president announced, "Roar Omega Roar wins the event!"

Mike and Sulley leaped across the finish line at the same time, still furious at each other. The crowd was laughing. A photographer called out, "Way to blow it, Oozmas!"

"Hey, second place isn't bad," Mike shouted back defensively.

Then he heard the council president say, "Second place, Jaws Theta Chi!"

"What?" Sulley cried in disbelief.

One of the fans yelled, "Your *whole team* has to cross the finish line!"

"Oh no," Sulley moaned. The last time he'd seen the Oozmas, they were sprawled across the tunnel floor.

"Third place, EEKs," said the council vice president. "Fourth place, PNKs . . . fifth place, HSS . . . and in last place, Oozma Kappa!"

"No, no!" Mike gasped, and then turned to see the last of the bruised and battered Oozmas finally cross the finish line.

"Oozma Kappa has been eliminated!" the Greek Council president announced.

Near panic, Mike stepped back and accidentally bumped into Dean Hardscrabble.

This time she gave him a satisfied grin. "Don't look so surprised, Mr. Wazowski," she said. "It would have taken a miracle for you to stay in."

Mike was nodding numbly when the council president suddenly said, "Attention, everyone, we have an announcement! Jaws Theta Chi has been disqualified. The use of illegal protective gel is cause for elimination."

"What? It's moisturizer!" said Big Red, one of the Jaws Theta Chi brothers. The crowd watched as a referee wiped a wad of goop off his arm and then poked him with an urchin. *Zap!* Big Red's arm swelled up like a balloon.

"It's a miracle! Oozma Kappa is back in the games!" the vice president announced.

Dean Hardscrabble's grin vanished. She glared at Mike. "Your luck will run out eventually," she told him, and stormed out of the sewer.

Mike looked at Sulley. Then he looked at the rest of the Oozmas, who were swollen, bruised, and waving at him pathetically. "This is going to be harder than I thought," he muttered.

The next day, Mike gathered the team out on the campus quad. Sulley leaned against a tree and watched as Mike had them line up military-style. "Okay, listen up, Oozmas!" Mike said. "We're going to have to start winning these things together, so that means I need each of you to pull your own weight."

"We've made a list of our strengths and weaknesses," Squishy said, smiling.

Don stepped forward. "In high school I was the master of the 'silent scare.' Why, I could sneak up on a field mouse in a pillow factory," he said as he got down on his hands and knees and began to creep across the sidewalk. But his suction cups made a loud *pop-pop-pop* sound. "Uh, sorry," Don said. "They get stickier when I'm sweaty."

Then Terri and Terry stepped up. One hand pulled out a deck of playing cards. "We're experts in the ancient craft of close-up magic," Terry said with an air of mystery as he waved the cards in front of them.

"It's all about misdirection," Terri explained. But just then, all the cards accidentally tumbled out of his sleeve and fell to the ground. Terry looked at his brother and gave an exasperated sigh.

"I have an extra toe," Art said. He laughed quietly and added, "Not with me, of course."

Mike could see that the boys needed some direction. "Guys, one slipup in the next event and we're goners. So for this to work, I need you to take every instinct you have and bury it deep, deep down."

"Done," Art said.

Mike nodded. "From now on, we are of one mind. *My* mind."

"Oh, please," Sulley said, rolling his eyes.

"I will tell you exactly what to do and how to do it," Mike continued.

Sulley made a face, but the Oozmas were completely on board. "Okay, Mike," they said. "That sure seems best."

Mike smiled at them and said, "Good. Give me fifty sneaks, right now, in place, let's go!"

As the Oozmas began to exercise, moving their oddly misshapen bodies, Sulley walked over to Mike and said, "You're wasting your time. We need a new team."

"We can't just get a new team," Mike replied. "I checked this morning, and it's against the rules."

"What if we disguise the new team to look like the old team?" Sulley asked hopefully.

"Oh, no. We are not cheating!" Mike said.

"It's not cheating," Sulley said, shaking his head. "I'm just, you know, leveling the playing field." Mike stared at him, and Sulley sighed. "Okay, so it's kind of cheating! But what do you want me to do? They're not exactly the scariest group in the world."

They both turned and looked at the Oozmas. Squishy was prancing around with a ladybug on his hand. "Oh, make a wish, everybody! Make a wish!"

Sulley gave Mike an annoyed look and walked off. "Where are you going?" Mike called after him. "We're training!"

"I'm a Sullivan!" Sulley called back. "You tell them what to do, but not me. Later, Coach."

Squishy suddenly sprung up behind Mike, who jumped into the air in surprise.

"AH!" he screamed. "Boy, we need to get you a bell!" Then he turned to the group. "Okay, Oozmas. Pop quiz: What's more dangerous than a human child?"

Art raised his hand and said, "Two human childs?"

Mike sighed. "No! A human adult! The next event is all about avoiding capture. So remember, do *exactly* what I do." Mike raised a foot and walked heel to toe, super-slow. The rest of the team nodded eagerly.

The library was absolutely quiet. Then, one by one, the Oozmas entered the huge room, weaving carefully around the tables. They followed Mike as well as they could, slowly, trying desperately not to make a sound. Heel to toe, heel to toe.

The second event of the Scare Games was under way. Across the room, flags were hanging from the arms of a tall statue. The goal of the event was to sneak across the library and remove a flag without alerting the librarian. She was as strict as they came: fifty feet tall, stern, with tentacles just waiting to grab noisy students. Her glasses were thick and her eyesight was poor, so she had to rely almost entirely on her sense of hearing. If team members made noise and attracted her attention, she'd toss them out. The last team with a flag left still dangling on the statue would be eliminated.

The Greek Council president and her vice president were watching from a side room overlooking the library. "We are at the halfway point of this event, and things are getting interesting," the president whispered to the crowd of onlookers. Everyone held their breath as the sorority girls from HSS reached the statue. The girls quickly snatched their flag and raced out of the library, passing the test. Of course, the RORs had already gotten their flag and passed, too. "Only two teams left," whispered the president. "Who will make it out with their flag and who will be eliminated?"

The vice president continued. "In a real scare, you do not want to get caught by a kid's parent," he whispered. "And in this event, you *do not* want to get caught by the librarian."

The librarian pressed a scaly finger to her lips and said, "*Shhh*. Quiet."

Terri scoffed and whispered, "I'm not afraid of some old librarian!" Just then, a student sneezed. The librarian whipped around toward the sound and seemed to become even larger and more terrifying. She grabbed the student in her tentacles.

"I said, *quiet!*" she snarled at the poor student.

Then she hurled the student upward, through a hole in the library's glass dome ceiling. The student flew into the air, then dropped down into the trees outside and landed in a stream.

Onlookers cheered and howled.

Mike looked at his frightened teammates and whispered, "Do exactly what I do." They nodded and crept slowly through the library, mimicking Mike's every move.

Sulley looked from his team to the EEKs, who were gaining speed. "FASTER!" Sulley whispered impatiently, trying to move his team along.

But Mike held up his hand. "Slow and steady," he told the team.

"Slow and steady," Art whispered, holding up his hand, imitating Mike exactly.

Sulley groaned in frustration as they each relayed the message down the line exactly as Mike had said it. Finally, he just couldn't take the Oozmas' snaillike pace a minute more. He bolted toward the flag, leaving his teammates behind.

Mike's eye went wide. "Sullivan!" he whispered.

"Sullivan!" Art whispered.

"Sullivan!" Terri and Terry whispered.

Mike shushed the team. "Shhh!" Art whispered to Terri and Terry.

"Shhh!" the brothers whispered to Don, who whispered it to Squishy.

Mike shook his head and sighed.

They all watched as Sulley ran to a ladder that was fastened on a track against the bookshelves. He climbed to the top and pushed the ladder so that it slid across the shelves toward the flag. Mike gasped as the librarian whipped her head around. She adjusted her glasses but didn't seem to notice Sulley. "Hmmm," she murmured suspiciously, and then returned to her work.

Sulley was near the flag now but not quite close enough. He inched forward, extending his arm toward the flag. He was almost touching it when the bottom of the ladder began coming off its tracks. A moment later, both Sulley and the ladder fell to the ground with a thunderous *CRASH!*

CHAPTER

18

The librarian rushed toward Sulley in a rage. Her huge tentacles were just about to wrap around his body when a loud *pop-pop-pop* noise sounded behind her. She whipped around, searching for the creature who dared destroy the silence of her library. It was Don.

He was crawling along the floor so that his tentacles would make a loud, sticky, suction-cup *pop* against the floor. He moved as quickly and as loudly as he could, popping up a storm! The librarian's tentacles suddenly shot in Don's direction. Don cringed and braced for the impact. But just before her slimy arms reached him, books began flying off the shelves in another part of the library.

"Over here!" Terri and Terry called out as they danced and loudly tossed books onto the floor. The librarian turned toward the two with fury in her eyes.

But then Art jumped on a table and began stomping his hairy purple feet. The librarian's attention immediately went to him.

The crowd watched in surprise. "Is that legal?" one of the onlookers asked.

"Oh yeah!" the vice president answered. "The only rule is don't get caught."

As the Oozmas and the librarian ran in every direction, Mike realized in horror that the EEKs were stacking themselves into a pyramid to get their flag. But before he could say anything, his teammates grabbed Mike and pulled him along. As the librarian lunged for them, her tail knocked the EEKs' pyramid to the floor. The Oozma gang leaped out the library door with an angry tentacle missing them by inches.

"Woo-hoo! We did it!" Art howled as the Oozmas landed in a heap.

Mike shook his head. "No, we didn't. We forgot the flag!" he said, exasperated.

Squishy suddenly popped up behind Mike. "*AHH!*" Mike screamed, surprised once again. Then Squishy reached behind his back and held up the flag.

The Oozmas cheered wildly, but Mike was stunned. "How . . . ?" he asked, confused.

Terri leaned toward Mike. With a wave of his arms and a mysterious smile, he said, "*Misdirection!*"

"Oozma Kappa moves on, and the EEKs

have been eliminated!" the Greek Council vice president announced. Dean Hardscrabble watched, expressionless, as the Oozma Kappas celebrated.

"We're OK! We're OK! We're OK!" they chanted.

As the Oozmas headed for home, they were giddy from their first real success. "I've never felt so alive!" Squishy said, his rosy cheeks redder than usual.

"We were awesome!" Terri and Terry agreed, nodding their heads enthusiastically.

But Sulley wasn't feeling it. "Look," he told them, "that wasn't real scaring."

"Oh, I disagree," Mike said. "I got to hand it to the guys; they came up with a very interesting solution. You, on the other hand, nearly got us eliminated. You should have stuck to my strategy."

"What strategy?" Sulley snapped. "That was a bunch of tiptoeing. Talk to me when we start the real scaring."

Mike was ready to argue the point when a car full of PNK sorority girls pulled up. "Hey, you guys going to the party?" a cute girl, who was leader of the PNKs, called out.

The Oozmas were stunned. "Oh, I think

you've got the wrong guys," Squishy said. "We don't get invited to—"

Mike quickly put a hand over Squishy's mouth. "Party?" Mike asked the girl.

"Yeah, the mid-games mixer at the RORs'. It's for the top scare teams. You're one of us now, right?"

"See you there!" another girl called out as the car pulled away.

The Oozmas looked at each other in shock. "Did you hear that? I can't believe it!" Don exclaimed.

"Uh-uh. Bad idea," Sulley said flatly.

But Mike wasn't about to pass it up. "People are finally seeing us as real Scarers. We are going!" he announced.

As they approached the ROR house, the Oozmas began to get cold feet. "Do young people still dance?" Don asked nervously. "'Cause my moves are a little rusty."

"Yeah, maybe this wasn't such a good idea," Terry said.

Squishy was looking a little panicked, too. "What if there's a lull in the conversation? I–I never know what to, uh, you know . . ."

". . . say?" Mike finished.

Squishy shook his head in astonishment.

"How are you so good at this?"

"You just took on an angry fifty-foot librarian, and you're afraid of a little party?" Mike put his arm around Squishy and gave him a nudge through the door. "In you go!" he said, and the rest of the Oozmas followed.

The ROR house was packed with monsters. They all turned when the Oozmas walked in. "Uh, hello," Squishy said nervously.

The crowd stared at them blankly. Then recognition swept through the group, and the party monsters hooted and shouted happily.

"Oozma Kappa!"

"These guys are crazy!"

"What you did today was insane!"

Mike looked at his team and smiled. "Oozma Kappa," he said, "tonight, we party like Scarers!"

Art quickly burst onto the dance floor, twisting and gyrating wildly.

Don also strutted his stuff, and Squishy started dancing with the PNKs, who seemed to really enjoy his company. "I've never stayed up this late in my life!" he told the girls.

Then Squishy spotted Sulley standing off to the side by himself and decided to lasso him onto the dance floor. Reluctantly, Sulley gave in and was pulled into the crowd. Soon, he was doing some monster moves of his own.

While the team danced, Mike wandered out into the hallway. Along the walls were portraits of past Scare Games winners. And there, set on a pedestal, was the Scare Games trophy, which the RORs had won last year. Looking at the golden trophy, Mike could see his own reflection. It made him look exactly as he felt: big and impressive. *I can win,* he thought.

Meanwhile, at the party, Johnny noticed the Oozmas on the dance floor. He whistled and called out to the crowd, "Hey, quiet! QUIET! On behalf of the RORs, we'd like to congratulate all the teams that have made it this far! Let's hear it for the PNKs! Looking good, ladies!"

The girls took a little bow, and the crowd cheered. "HSS!" Johnny continued. "Very creepy!" After more cheering, he turned back to the crowd. "And finally, the surprise team of the scare games, OOZMA KAPPA! Come on over, guys."

The crowd parted and a spotlight hit the Oozmas. "Let's hear it for Oozma Kappa!" Johnny cried.

The Oozmas smiled. But suddenly, without warning, gallons of paint were tossed into their midst, splattering the entire group.

The crowd was confused, but Johnny started

laughing. Then a machine shot glitter confetti at the Oozmas and a ROR tossed a bucket of flowers. "The most adorable monsters on campus!" Johnny howled. Then he shouted, "Release the stuffed animals!"

Another ROR brother yanked on a rope that was connected to a net. A huge pile of cute little stuffed animals dropped on top of the Oozmas. A camera clicked and caught the Oozmas' glittery, horrified expressions.

⎯⎯M⎯⎯

The next day, the humiliating photo was on the front page of the school newspaper. Mike was doing his best to keep his team's morale high, but it wasn't easy. "Don't worry. Nobody reads the school newspaper," Mike said as they walked to class.

"Yeah, but I'm pretty sure they read the quad," Art replied. Mike looked up and saw the entire quad plastered with the same embarrassing photo. Students were looking at the photos and laughing. And just when it felt like it couldn't get worse, Mike and the Oozmas saw a monster flying through the air—pulling a banner with the words "Cutie Kappa" on it.

Up ahead, Johnny and the RORs were busy

selling T-shirts and mugs featuring the Oozma photo. Mike was furious. "Hey, what are you doing?" he demanded.

"Raising a little money for charity," Johnny replied with a laugh.

"I want you to stop making us look like fools," Mike said angrily.

Johnny held up a copy of the *Campus Roar* and pointed at the Oozmas' ridiculous picture. "You're making yourselves look like fools," he said. "Let's be honest, guys. You're never gonna be *real* Scarers, because real Scarers look like us."

Then Johnny flipped the newspaper over and pointed to a Monsters, Inc., ad in the classifieds. "But hey, if you really want to work at a scare floor, they're always hiring in the mail room." Johnny and the crowd laughed.

Sulley couldn't take any more. Fuming, he turned and walked away. The Oozmas, sad and dejected, were close behind. "Hey, hold up!" Mike called after them. "Don't listen to him! We just need to keep trying—"

Sulley turned and faced Mike. "No, you need to stop trying! We're just embarrassing ourselves. You can train monsters like this all you want, but you can't change who they are."

As the Oozmas watched Sulley leave, Don turned to Mike. "We appreciate everything you've done, but he's right. No matter how much we train, we'll never look like them." He sighed. "We're built for other things."

The Oozmas left, following Sulley back to their house. Their heads were all hanging low when Mike got an idea. "Guys!" he said, a new light in his eyes. "I've been doing this all wrong. We're going on a little field trip!"

It was late when Mike piled all the Oozmas into Ms. Squibbles's car—with Ms. Squibbles driving. After a long drive, Mike told her to pull into a dark parking lot. "Thanks, Mom!" Squishy said as the group climbed out and stretched.

Ms. Squibbles waved. "Have fun, kids! I'll just be here listening to my tunes." She rolled up her window, and the car began to vibrate with the thud of heavy metal music.

Art looked around. "So where are we?" he asked Mike.

All the Oozmas followed Mike as he walked toward a large gate and gazed upward. "The big leagues," Mike said solemnly.

Everyone looked up and saw the sign: MONSTERS, INC.

"Holy roly-poly!" Don said, awestruck. Even Sulley was stunned.

Mike held up a pair of wire cutters and the Oozmas gasped. "We're not stopping here," Mike told them. Moments later, he had cut a big hole in the wire fence—right next to the No Trespassing sign.

"This is crazy! We're gonna get arrested!" Squishy whispered as Mike led the group up a ladder and onto the roof of Monsters, Inc.

"*Shh!*" Mike said, leading them toward a big window.

As the group peered through the window, everyone's eyes went wide. "Whoa!" someone exclaimed. They were looking down onto a real scare floor, full of Scarers going in and out of active doors to the human world.

"Take a good look, fellas," Mike said, pointing to the Scarers below. "See what they all have in common?"

Squishy stared hard at the workers down on the scare floor. They were different shapes, colors, and sizes. "No, not really," Squishy said finally, feeling confused.

"Exactly!" Mike exclaimed. "There's no one type of Scarer. The best Scarers use their differences to their advantage."

"Wow," Squishy said, watching a blobby Scarer expand himself to enormous size.

"Terri, look!" Terry called to his brother. They both stared as a three-headed Scarer came out from an active door.

Sulley was impressed, too. He watched the Scarers for a while, then glanced over at Mike with new respect. Maybe Mike was right.

Don gasped as he noticed an older monster on the floor. "Hey, look at that old fella racking up the big numbers!"

Mike smiled. "Don, that 'old fella' is Earl 'The Terror' Thompson!"

"What?" Sulley said, astounded. "Where?" Then he laughed. "Wow! That's really him! I still have his rookie card!"

"Me too!" Mike said, and for the first time, they realized they had something in common. "You collect scare cards, huh?" Mike asked.

"Yep," Sulley replied proudly. "Four hundred and fifty of 'em."

"Impressive," Mike said, nodding. "I have six thousand. Still in mint condition. But, you know, four-fifty's pretty good, too."

Squishy, inspired by what he saw on the floor, made a scary face and let out a roar. "Hey, look at me," he said, "I'm Earl 'The Terror' Thompson!"

"Hey, that was pretty good!" Art said.

Mike and Sulley watched the Oozmas grow excited as they realized they might actually achieve their dreams.

Then Sulley turned to Mike with a sigh. "I've been a real jerk, haven't I?"

"So have I," Mike admitted. "But it's not too late. We could be a great team. We just to need to start working together—"

"Hey! What are you doing up there?" a security guard yelled.

The entire group froze in surprise. Then Art panicked. "I can't go back to jail!" he cried, and raced away across the rooftop. Mike and the other Oozmas followed.

"They're right behind us!" Don cried as Sulley pulled him along. The gang hustled up a ladder, hoping to hide on a higher rooftop. But they were too slow.

"There they are, up there!" the security guard shouted. A whole group of guards was chasing them now. "Get 'em!"

Mike gasped as the guards climbed the ladder, hot on their tails and tentacles. Mike led the Oozmas to a ledge and jumped to a lower rooftop. Squishy was the last to jump. Terrified, he teetered on the ledge, then fell. Sulley reached out his long arm and caught him just in time. "Thanks, brother," Squishy gasped.

Sulley put Squishy on his shoulders and ran. "Don't mention it," Sulley said as he caught up to Mike and the other Oozma Kappas.

It wasn't long before Don was out of breath and falling behind. "I'm fine, really," Don said, gasping. "It's just a little heart attack." Sulley picked Don up, too, and kept running.

"Stop right there!" a guard shouted. "Don't move!" But Sulley, who was now carrying all the Oozmas, plowed through. He jumped to the ground and sprinted to the car.

"Mom! Start the car!" Squishy yelled as they ducked out through the fence.

Ms. Squibbles lowered her window and smiled. "What, dear?"

"Start the car!" Squishy howled. "THE CAR! Start the car!"

Ms. Squibbles smiled. "Oh, okay," she said. Mike and the Oozmas piled in.

"Mom, go!" Squishy said as the guards climbed through the hole after them.

"Seat belts," Ms. Squibbles reminded her son and his friends with a smile.

The Oozmas frantically buckled up as the guards moved closer. "Okay," Squishy panted. "Go!"

"Does anyone want gum?" Ms. Squibbles asked.

"JUST DRIVE!" Squishy hollered. But it was

too late. The guards had caught up to the car. Desperate, Mike reached his foot over to the gas pedal and floored it. The car screeched out of the Monsters, Inc., parking lot.

"*AAAAHHH!*" the Oozmas screamed as the car tore down the road. Then they all started laughing.

"That was awesome!" Terri said, and they looked back to see angry guards shaking their fists in the distance.

"Let's break in somewhere else!" Art cried.

=M=

Back home at the Oozma Kappa house, the Oozmas had a completely different attitude from earlier that day. Inspired, the group started training for the Scare Games with a confidence and determination they'd never had before. Ms. Squibbles sewed them yellow-and-green sweaters, for their fraternity colors. When Sulley and Mike put on their sweaters and Oozma hats, they exchanged a thumbs-up. They were a team!

From then on, all the Oozmas were up at six a.m. They were out on the quad practicing scaring drills every day. "Scary feet! Scary feet!" Mike shouted to them as they slithered, raced, and crawled across the field.

In the distance, Johnny and Chet watched the Oozmas practicing and shook their heads. The third Scare Games event was Don't Scare the Teen, and they were sure the Oozma Kappas didn't have a chance.

CHAPTER

21

On the day of the event, the Oozmas anxiously gathered at the entrance of a large maze. As Mike explained, "This event is all about scaring the young kids while avoiding the older kids." It was a race with a twist: as contestants sprinted through the maze, cardboard pop-ups of children would appear. The trick was to roar at just the little children pop-ups, not the teens.

The crowd cheered as Art ran through the maze first. He sped around a corner and encountered a cardboard pop-up teenager. Art ducked behind a corner until a light on the teen turned green. That meant the Oozmas scored a point.

Squishy ran through next. A cardboard child popped up and Squishy let out a *ROAR!* Another green light flashed. The Oozmas scored again!

The RORs emerged from the maze in first place. But the Oozmas came out second, beating both the HSS sorority and the PNKs. The PNKs were eliminated, and the OKs were still in the Games. The Oozma fans screamed, "Go OK!"

The next Scare Games event would focus on hiding. The team hit the books hard and learned how each Oozma could make the most of his individual abilities. To help Don understand this concept, Mike put a helmet on him and had Sulley throw him at a wall. Don screamed as he flew through the air—but when he hit, he stuck tight! Thrilled, Don continued climbing stealthily up the wall, using the suction cups on his tentacle arms.

One by one, the Oozmas were finding their strengths. Sulley listened carefully as Mike read passages from scaring manuals. It was the first time Sulley had ever cared about anything in a book. But he could see that Mike's strategy was working. When the night of the next challenge arrived, even Sulley felt the Oozmas were ready.

The event was called Hide-and-Sneak and required the remaining three teams to hide inside the ROR house. Any time the referee spotted a monster, that player was out. If the referee passed by, the monster could run out of the house and be counted for his or her team. A crowd gathered outside the windows of the ROR house to watch the game unfold.

Quickly, the competitors ran into the house and found their hiding places. The referee, a monster with multiple eyes, carefully entered the house. His flashlight quickly landed on a set of tentacles beneath a curtain. The tentacles pulled back. But it was too late. The referee yanked the curtain aside and found a HSS sorority girl. "You're out!" he shouted.

Then he moved his flashlight to the fireplace. The steely-eyed ref noticed loose debris falling from the chimney. He shined the light up and a different HSS sorority sister fell into the soot. "Tough luck, Kris Kringle," he said.

Then the referee walked across the room, stepping right over Sulley, who had disguised himself as a bear rug. As the referee moved off toward the next area of the house, Sulley stood up and ran outside. Continuing, the referee walked under Don, who went unnoticed, clinging to the ceiling with his suction cups.

The crowd waiting outside saw the RORs come out the front door first, followed closely by the Oozma Kappas. The Oozma fans went crazy.

At the end of the challenge, the Greek Council president addressed the crowd. "We're down to two remaining teams: the four-time defending champions, Roar Omega Roar . . . and Oozma Kappa!"

The vice president added, "Get plenty of rest, because tomorrow night you finally get to scare in front of the whole school!"

As the crowd began to break up, a group of fans approached the Oozma Kappas. "You guys are awesome!" one student said. "You've got to teach us your moves."

"Well, then you're going to want to talk to this guy," Don said, proudly pointing to Mike.

Mike was surprised and pleased by the attention.

Sulley smiled as he watched Mike enjoy his moment in the sun. Then he spotted Dean Hardscrabble and walked over. This time Sulley wasn't so arrogant. "Dean Hardscrabble?" he said humbly. "When we get back into the Scaring Program, I hope there's no hard feelings."

She turned to Sulley with a strange look. "Tomorrow, each of you must prove that you are undeniably scary. And I know for a fact that one of you is not." She turned, her gaze falling on Mike.

"No," Sulley replied. "You're wrong. He works harder than anyone."

"But do you think he's scary?" she asked.

"He's the heart and soul of the team," Sulley answered.

"Do *you* think he's scary?" she repeated.

Sulley looked at Mike, grinning and enthusiastic, and his shoulders slumped. Dean Hardscrabble smiled coldly, as if to say *That's what I thought.* She turned and walked away.

Back in their little room at the Oozma Kappa house, Sulley stared at the ceiling while Mike sat on his bunk below. "We're gonna win this thing tomorrow, Sull, I can feel it!" Mike said happily, holding his old MU hat.

Sulley leaned over his bunk and said, "Hey, Mike? You've given me a lot of really great tips. I'd love to return the favor sometime."

"Oh yeah, sure. Anytime," Mike replied.

Sulley jumped down from his bunk and cleared the furniture from the middle of the room. "We're doing this now?" Mike asked.

Sulley picked up Mike's scaring textbook and tossed it. "Okay, you've memorized every textbook, every scare theory, and that's great. But now it's time to forget all that. Just reach deep down and let the scary out," he said seriously.

Mike stared at him for a moment. "Huh, just feel it," he said.

"Exactly," Sulley replied. "Go wild."

Mike let out a roar. "Good," Sulley said, "but bigger!"

Mike roared at Sulley with everything he had. Ms. Squibbles suddenly shouted, "Boys! It's a school night!"

Mike was breathing hard. "So how was it?" he asked.

Sulley smiled and held up his big hand. "Up top," he said, and Mike high-fived him. Mike and Sulley climbed back into their bunks.

"Ha-ha!" Mike said happily. "It did feel different. I feel like it's all coming together." He grabbed his beloved MU hat. "Yep, this time tomorrow, the whole school is finally going to see what Mike Wazowski can do."

"You're darn right," Sulley said, staring at the ceiling. He hoped he sounded like he meant it.

The next day, MU's stadium was packed with cheering students. The Greek Council president stood onstage and addressed the crowd. "Welcome to the final competition of the Scare Games!" she shouted.

Then the Oozmas came out in their team caps and sweaters. They waved, and the crowd went wild. As the RORs took the stage, the Greek Council president said to the teams, "It's time to see how terrifying you really are—in the scare simulators!"

She indicated two scare simulators on the field, one for each team. Competitors would go head to head. "But be warned," the president added, "each simulated scare has been set to the highest difficulty level!"

"The highest level?" Squishy said nervously.

Mike felt nervous, too. But he took a breath and turned to his team. "Okay, just like we planned. I'll go first, then Don."

"Hold on," Sulley interjected. "Mike's the one who started all this. And I think it's only right if he's the one who finishes it. I think you should go last."

Mike looked up in surprise. But the others quickly agreed. "Yeah!" said Don.

"Good idea," Terry added.

"Right on, man!" Art said heartily.

Mike was flattered. "All right," he told his teammates. "Don? You okay starting first?"

"Sure," Don replied. The Oozmas formed a circle and stacked their hands. Mike placed his on top, and they cheered, "Ooooooozma Kappa!"

Don ran to the Oozma simulator while Reggie, a ROR brother, raced to the RORs' simulator. They waited for the light that would signal them to start.

"Take it easy on grandpa!" Johnny yelled from the sidelines as the light outside the simulators flashed from red to green. It was time to GO!

Don carefully opened the door of the simulator and entered the dark room. The crowd watched on the stadium's Jumbotron as Don stealthily dodged the toys on the floor.

Meanwhile, Reggie crept into his simulator room and immediately stepped on a rubber ducky. He gasped as the duck squeaked, and the sim-kid sat up in bed. Reggie's plan was thrown off, but he quickly recovered and *ROARED!*

"*AHHHHH!*" the sim-kid screamed.

At the same time, inside the Oozma simulator, Don's sim-kid was also sitting up. But Don was clinging to the ceiling above. Suddenly, Don swooped down toward the bed, hanging by one arm as he *ROARED!* The sim-kid screamed his sim lungs out.

When Reggie and Don exited the simulators, Don's scream can was fuller than Reggie's by an inch! Don looked at the RORs and smiled. "Good luck, kids," he said smugly. Reggie was stunned.

Next, Terri and Terry walked up to the simulator door. Their opponent for the RORs was Chet, who glared at the brothers. But Terri and Terry stayed upbeat. "LET'S DO THIS!" they shouted as the light turned green.

Inside the ROR simulator, Chet snuck up to the bed and let out a fearsome *ROARRRRR!* Johnny cheered as the scoreboard showed Chet's scream-can results. It was going to be a hard score to beat.

Inside the Oozma simulator, the sim-kid sat up in bed. The kid spotted what looked like the silhouette of a human dad standing in the room. The sim-kid was about to lie back down when the silhouette suddenly split into a looming two-headed creature. The sim-kid screamed in terror as both heads roared! Their scare came in just below Chet's!

Next came Squishy. The sim-kid was lying in his bed when his closet door slowly opened. The child looked over at the door, but now it was shut. Then an eerie shadow passed the window. The sim-kid was about to lie back down when it saw Squishy lying in bed beside him. The sim-kid screamed—and Squishy's scream can filled more than halfway!

"Wooo!" Ms. Squibbles cheered.

Art entered the simulator room next. He was competing against a four-armed bug monster from the RORs. Art carefully crept to the foot of the sim-kid's bed. Then he jumped onto the end of the bed and struck a strange yoga pose. He warbled a creepy roar, and his scream can filled up halfway.

That was a good score, but not great—and the Oozmas were falling further and further behind. The team was disappointed, but they rallied as they realized it was time to bring out their strongest Scarers: Sulley and Mike!

Sulley approached the Oozma simulator, cracked his huge knuckles, and entered the room. In the ROR simulator, Randy also entered, climbing the side of the room and disappearing against the wall.

Sulley carefully crept up to the bed, slowly looming up and over the sim-kid. Then he let out the most ferocious *ROARRRRR* of the day!

In the other simulator, Randy was about to start his own scare when the sound of Sulley's roar knocked him off the wall. Randy fell to the floor, blended into a heart pattern on the bedroom rug, and let out a meager yelp. The sim-kid responded with a very short scream.

"It's all tied up!" the Greek Council vice president announced, indicating the scoreboard as Sulley and Randy emerged from their simulators. Against Randy's poor performance, Sulley had pulled the OKs up to the same score as the RORs.

Johnny and the RORs were furious with Randy. "You stink, Boggs!" Chet told him.

Randy seethed as he watched the Oozmas celebrate. "That's the last time I lose to you, Sullivan," he muttered.

"Worthington and Wazowski to the starting line!" the Greek Council vice president announced.

All eyes were on Mike as he marched to the starting line next to Johnny. The light turned green and both ran to their simulators. As they entered their doors, Johnny ran right to the bed while Mike took his time, distracting his sim-kid with a scratch on the bedpost.

Johnny went straight to the bed with a huge *ROARRR!* The sim-kid screamed, giving Johnny almost a full scream can. Johnny stepped out of the simulator and strutted like a champion as the crowd chanted, "ROR! ROR! ROR!"

Inside the Oozma simulator, Mike crouched by the bed, contemplating his next move. He knew it was all up to him. He thought about everything he'd been told over the years . . . leading up to Sulley's advice: *Let the scary out!* Mike focused his energy and leaped onto the bed, letting out his best, most intense *ROARRRRR!*

The sim-kid screamed—and Mike's scream can filled to the top! The crowd went wild! The Oozmas were the winners of the Scare Games!

The OKs jumped up and down happily as the crowd cheered, "Oozma! Oozma!" and Sulley shouted, "We're in the Scaring Program!" Ms. Squibbles was hugging everyone. She hugged Don, but his tentacles stuck to her. They both pulled away, slightly embarrassed.

"Oh, pardon me, there, Ms. Squibbles," Don said.

Ms. Squibbles batted her five blue eyes and blushed. "It's Sheri," she said sweetly as the Oozmas hoisted Mike onto their shoulders.

At last, the celebration began to wind down, but the Oozma Kappas felt that all their dreams had come true. They had accepted their trophy and were basking in the glory of being winners. As they finished shaking hands with the crowd, one fan shouted, "You rule!"

Don grinned. "I have never ruled before," he said. Sulley laughed as he looked for Mike in the crowd.

"Hey, Wazowski!" Sulley shouted, finally spotting Mike near the Oozmas' simulator. "Come on, let's go, you maniac! We're celebrating!"

But Mike didn't respond. He seemed dazed. "Mike?" Sulley asked.

"I did it," Mike said in an awed tone. He walked into the simulator and stared at the sim-kid. "I can't believe it. I'm going to be a Scarer."

Sulley smiled. "Yeah. Yeah, you are."

Mike turned toward the sim-kid and said, "You hear that? Get plenty of rest, kiddo, 'cause you haven't seen the last of Mike Wazowski." Mike playfully threw his hands in the air and said, "BOO!"

The sim-kid shot straight up in bed and screamed. Mike turned to see the scream can fill to the top. "I knew I was scary," Mike said, confused, "but I didn't know I was *that* scary."

"Yeah," Sulley replied. "We're so scary, I guess we broke it."

A dark thought suddenly passed through Mike's round head. He walked over to the sleeping sim-kid and snapped his fingers. *"AHHHHH!"* the sim-kid screamed, and shot out of bed again.

Mike lifted the bed skirt and took a look at the settings on the control panel. Sulley shifted nervously. "Come on," he said to Mike, "I don't think you should be messing with that."

But Mike looked closer at the gauges. He noticed that the settings for each round in the simulator were set on high—except for the last one. His own settings were on the lowest, not the highest, level. All at once, it dawned on him: the simulator had been rigged.

Mike turned to Sulley. "Did *you* do this?" he asked.

Sulley struggled for an answer. Finally, he said, "I . . . Yes, I did." He watched Mike's face drop. "But you don't understand."

Mike was heartbroken. "Why?"

Sulley hung his head and sighed. "You know, just in case."

Mike knew all too well. "You don't think I'm scary," he said, stunned. "You're just like Hardscrabble and everyone else."

"Well, what was I supposed to do?" Sulley replied, defending himself against Mike's anger. "Let the whole team fail because you don't have it?"

The words shot Mike through the heart. He stared at Sulley for a moment. Then he stormed off.

Sulley looked to one side and saw the rest of the Oozmas staring at him in shock. They had been standing near the simulator and had heard everything.

Squishy sadly set the trophy down on the ground. Then he and the other Oozmas walked away, hurt and confused.

Sulley stood alone on the stage, trying to

process it all. He picked up the trophy and numbly walked across campus.

Johnny and the RORs spotted him and crowded around. Johnny slapped Sulley on the back. "Looks like I was wrong about you," Johnny said, throwing a ROR jacket over Sulley's big shoulders. "You're one of us after all."

Sulley saw Dean Hardscrabble up ahead. He stared for a moment, and then a look of resolve came into his eyes. He handed both trophy and jacket to Johnny. As the RORs watched in surprise, he left them behind and strode purposefully toward Hardscrabble.

At the same time, Mike was walking through the halls of MU's door tech building, heading to the door lab. As he passed a group of students exiting the lab, he casually lifted a key card from a backpack. Looking around to make sure no one was watching, he quickly swiped the card and waited for the security light above the lab door to turn green.

Out on the quad, Sulley finally caught up with Dean Hardscrabble and quickly explained how he'd rigged the simulator. "You did what?" she asked, unbelieving.

"My team had nothing to do with it," Sulley said. "It was all me. . . . I cheated."

Dean Hardscrabble folded her bat-winged arms across her chest. "I want you off campus by tomorrow," she ordered. "You are a disgrace to this university and your family name."

"Yes, ma'am," Sulley replied softly.

Suddenly, a security guard ran by. "Someone's broken into the door lab!" he shouted.

Dean Hardscrabble immediately launched into the air and flew toward the door tech building. Sulley watched her go, but then he realized that this news was no coincidence. "Oh no," he murmured. It had to be Mike!

Meanwhile, in the lab, Mike placed a scream can in its station next to a door to the human world. He was determined to prove to himself and to everyone else that he was scary, and not with some fake sim-kid but with the real thing.

Mike could hear security guards shouting outside the lab. But he had blocked the door so they couldn't enter. He turned the knob of the door in front of him and calmly stepped into the human world.

Seeing a child in bed, Mike quietly approached his target. He ruffled the curtains and crept alongside the bed, building his scare. Sensing something in the room, the child slowly sat up and looked around. Mike leaped toward her and *ROARED!*

The little girl looked at Mike. Still sleepy, she smiled at him and said, "You look funny."

"What?" Mike asked, stunned. Then he heard someone cough. Mike looked around and saw that he was in a cabin full of beds. A banner on the wall read CAMP TEAMWORK.

Mike rolled his one eye in disbelief as the little girl began to wake all her bunkmates. "My imaginary friend is here!" she told them excitedly. "He's a funny little green guy!" Mike gasped as the kids started coming closer.

Back in the monster world, Dean Hardscrabble had entered into the door lab and was guarding Mike's door. "No one goes through that door until the Child Detection Agency team arrives!"

Sulley and the Oozmas were at the front of the crowd. Sulley was ready to plow through to get to Mike, but the Oozmas held him back. "James, wait!" Squishy said. "We can help."

Don stepped forward. "Just leave it to old Don Carlton, 'Master of Sales.'" Don confidently strolled over to Dean Hardscrabble. "Pardon me," he said smoothly. "Today is your lucky day. How many times have you asked yourself—"

Dean Hardscrabble took one look at Don and said, "Arrest him."

Sulley cringed as the door tech guards immediately pounced on Don. "UP AGAINST THE WALL, POPS!" one guard shouted as they tackled him.

In the confusion, Sulley noticed that the path to the door was clear. Dean Hardscrabble saw him out of the corner of her eye and screamed, "Sullivan! Don't you dare!" But it was too late. Sulley slipped through the door before anyone could stop him.

Cautiously, Sulley crept through the dark cabin, which was now empty. "Mike? Mike?"

he whispered. Looking up, he saw the camp's banner, but there was no sign of Mike.

Then he heard voices outside and peeked through the window. A group of human kids were gathered around their camp counselors. Sulley heard one counselor tell a camp ranger, "They're calling it an alien."

"It was!" the kids clamored. "We saw a little green guy!"

Sulley saw the counselors' flashlights, so he ducked through a torn screen in a window. As he ran off into the dark woods, a couple of the rangers spotted him. "Bear!" one of them shouted. "Bear in the camp!"

Sulley jumped down into a gulley, evading the camp rangers' flashlights. He fought his way through some thick brush. Finally, he looked around and saw that he was by a lake. And there, sitting alone on the bank, was Mike.

"Mike!" Sulley gasped. Mike didn't look up. "Come on, buddy," Sulley said. "Let's get you out of here."

But Mike just silently stared at the water. Sulley could see he was hurting. "Mike?" Sulley said with a sigh. "This is all my fault. I'm sorry."

Mike shook his head in despair. "You were right. They weren't scared of me. I did everything right. I wanted it more than anyone. And I thought if I wanted it enough, I could show everybody that Mike Wazowski is something special. But I'm just not." Mike regarded his reflection in the lake.

"Look, Mike, I know how you feel," Sulley said.

Mike suddenly stood up. "Don't do that. Please don't do that. You do NOT know how

I feel!" His voice began to rise. "You'll never know what it's like to fail, because you were born a Sullivan!"

"Yeah, I'm a Sullivan," Sulley answered. "I'm the Sullivan who flunked every test and got kicked out of the program. I was so afraid to let everyone down that I cheated and lied." He sighed. "Yeah, I'll never know how you feel, but you're not the only failure here." He sighed. "I'm scary, Mike, but most of the time . . . I'm terrified."

"How come you never told me that before?" Mike asked, seeing Sulley in a whole different way.

"Because," Sulley said, shuffling his feet, "we weren't friends before."

Just then, flashlights flickered through the trees. Mike and Sulley heard dogs barking. Mike hid behind a bush as a flashlight grazed over Sulley. "This way!" one of the rangers shouted as Sulley took off. The rangers were close behind.

Fleeing, Sulley tried to climb up a slippery hill. The flashlights were getting closer. Mike appeared at the top of the steep hill. He lowered a tree limb over the side and helped Sulley climb to the top.

Together, Mike and Sulley raced through the

dark woods and back into the cabin. But when they opened the closet door, all they saw were brooms and buckets.

"No!" Mike cried. They had lost access to the monster world.

Inside the door lab, Dean Hardscrabble had just pressed her finger on the power button and shut the door down. Don saw the light above the door go out and shouted, "They're still in there!"

"Until the CDA arrives, this door stays off," Hardscrabble ordered.

The Oozmas knew it was a death sentence for Mike and Sulley. Squishy frantically made a dash for the door, but the guards easily took him down. "Enough!" Dean Hardscrabble shouted. "I want this room cleared, now!"

Meanwhile, in the human world, Mike and Sulley were in a panic. They could hear the humans outside the cabin, coming closer and closer.

"We gotta get outta here!" Sulley whispered desperately. He headed toward a window.

"No!" Mike said. "Let them come."

Sulley already had one foot out the window when he realized Mike wasn't following him. "If we scare them," Mike explained, "I mean *really* scare them, we could generate enough scream to power the door from this side."

"What are you talking about?" Sulley asked.

"I've read every book about scaring ever written," Mike said. "This could work!"

Sulley fought to keep from screaming. "They're ADULTS! I can't do this!"

"Yes, you can," Mike replied. "Just follow my lead."

Sulley pulled his big foot back into the room and listened to Mike's plan.

Moments later, the doorknob turned. The camp rangers entered the dark, empty cabin and aimed their flashlights in every direction. For a moment, there was silence. Then a fan in the corner turned on by itself. The humans jumped in surprise . . . and the fan slowly stopped. A curtain at the side of the room rustled, and a window shutter clattered open and shut.

Up in the rafters, Mike and Sulley gave each other a thumbs-up. A moment later, the rangers turned and saw a strange, small dark form whisk through the shadows. A record started playing backward. The rangers were becoming unnerved by the eerie music when they heard the sound of claws tearing through wood. They shined their flashlights on the walls and found them covered with deep claw marks.

Sulley was smiling and blowing the sawdust off his big hands. He waited for his cue from Mike and then placed a windup doll on the floor.

"Ma-ma. Ma-ma," the doll said creepily. It walked into a bedpost and toppled over.

"Now to Phase Two," Mike whispered. Sulley nodded and pushed one of the bunk beds. It hit another bed, and then another, until the entire row of beds fell like dominoes, crashing to the floor. The rangers began screaming wildly.

Back inside the door tech lab, Dean Hardscrabble saw the red light over the door flicker. She stared at it, baffled.

The terrified rangers ran for the cabin door, but the beds were blocking the exit. Mike nodded at Sulley, who jumped down from the rafters. His huge blue body loomed over the rangers as he let out the meanest, lowest growl he could muster. The roar hit the rangers with the force of an oncoming train. The trapped rangers screamed! Mike could see the closet door begin to glow bright red.

Dean Hardscrabble stared at the door in disbelief. "Impossible!" she gasped as she shielded her eyes from the blindingly bright red light. Then the scream can at the door filled to the top. She spun around at the sound of scream cans filling and rattling on the shelves.

Dean Hardscrabble covered her face as the cans began shooting off the shelf in every direction. She stared, dumbstruck, as the door exploded and Mike and Sulley burst in amid a cloud of smoke and debris. Sulley rubbed his eyes and stepped over the broken door.

"How . . . how did you do this?" Hardscrabble demanded to know as Mike picked up his battered MU cap from the rubble.

Sulley shrugged and looked down at Mike. "Don't ask me," he told the dean.

Mike looked up at Dean Hardscrabble's stunned expression. For once, he felt speechless.

Later that day, after their disciplinary hearing, Mike and Sulley returned to the OK fraternity house. The other Oozmas were eager to hear what had happened.

"Expelled?" Don gasped.

Mike nodded. "Yeah, we really messed up." He looked at his Oozma brothers and said, "I'm sorry, guys. You'd be in the Scaring Program right now if it weren't for us."

The Oozmas stared at Mike and Sulley awkwardly, as if they knew something else. "What?" Sulley finally asked them.

"Well," Don began, "it's the gosh-darndest thing. Hardscrabble's letting us back in the Scaring Program."

"She was impressed with our performance at the games . . . so she invited us to join next semester!" Terri and Terry continued.

Sulley started laughing. "Congratulations, guys!"

"And that's not the only good news," Don said eagerly. "Sheri and I are engaged!"

Mike and Sulley looked at each other in confusion. "Who's Sheri?" Sulley asked.

"She's my mom," Squishy said, embarrassed.

Ms. Squibbles suddenly waddled up to the group. "Well, if it isn't my two favorite fellas!" she said, beaming at Don and Squishy. Ms. Squibbles nuzzled up to Don, smiling. "Come here and give me some sugar."

Squishy looked like he was ready to die. "So uncomfortable . . . ," he muttered.

"Aw, come on, Scott," Don said to Squishy. "I don't want you to think of me as your new dad. After all, we're fraternity brothers first. Just think of me as your big brother who's marrying your mother."

"This is so weird," Squishy said, cringing.

Mike and Sulley packed their bags and said their farewells to their Oozma brothers. "Promise you'll keep in touch," Don said, handing Mike his business card. The word "sales" was scratched out and the words "scare student" had been written in.

Mike smiled. "You're the scariest bunch of monsters I ever met," he told them as they hugged their last good-bye. "Don't let anyone tell you different."

"So, what now?" Sulley asked as he and Mike

walked toward the campus gate.

"You know, this is the first time in my life I don't really have a plan," Mike replied.

But Sulley wasn't worried. "You're the great Mike Wazowski!" he said. "You'll come up with something."

Mike shrugged as his bus arrived. "I think it's time I leave the greatness to other monsters. I'm okay just being okay. So long, Sul." He shook his friend's hand and climbed aboard the bus.

Sulley nodded. "So long, Mike."

The bus pulled away. Mike stared out at the university he was leaving behind.

Suddenly, two blue hands reached into the window. "Wazowski!" Sulley yelled, and then fell away.

"Stop the bus!" Mike yelled. He jumped off and ran back to see Sulley lying on the ground. "Are you crazy?" Mike asked, rushing up to him.

Sulley sat up and looked his friend in the eye. There was something he needed to say. "I don't know a single Scarer who can do what you do," Sulley said. "I know when everyone sees us together, they think I'm the one running the show, but the truth is I've been riding your coattails since day one. You made the deal with Hardscrabble, you took a hopeless team and made them champions. All I did was catch a pig. Mike, you're not scary, not even a little . . . but you are fearless."

Mike stopped in his tracks. He'd never thought of himself, little Mike Wazowski, as fearless.

"And if Hardscrabble can't see that," Sulley continued, "then she can just—"

"I can just *what*?" Dean Hardscrabble said, approaching from behind him. Sulley and Mike gaped at her. "Careful, Mr. Sullivan. I was just beginning to like you."

"Sorry," Sulley said quickly.

Dean Hardscrabble held up a copy of the *Campus Roar*. "Well, it seems you made the front page again." Mike and Sulley sheepishly looked at a photo of the CDA hauling them away from the shattered door lab.

Dean Hardscrabble couldn't help but smile a little as she handed the paper to Mike. "The two of you have done something together no one has ever done before," she said. "You surprised me. Perhaps I should keep an eye out for more surprises like you in my Scaring Program." She began to walk away, then turned around. "And, Mr. Wazowski? Keep surprising people." Then she flew off.

Mike watched as she disappeared into the sky. Then he looked at the newspaper she'd left behind and noticed something on the back page. Suddenly, he smiled at Sulley. "There's still a way we could work at a scare floor," he said, holding up the Help Wanted section.

EPILOGUE

"**I** can't believe it! We work at Monsters, Incorporated!" Mike said to Sulley. They both proudly wore their MI hard hats. "I bet we break the all-time record in our first year!"

"Mike, we're in the mail room," Sulley reminded him.

"Oh, I know," he replied, smiling and sorting envelopes. "I'm talking about the record for letters delivered!"

"Hey, enough chatter, you two! Get back to work!" the mail manager barked.

"We're right on it, Mr. Shrill!" Mike said. Then he turned to Sulley. "The team of Wazowski and Sullivan is going to change the world, starting today! Say 'Scream!'" He held up a camera and snapped a picture of the two of them working.

And Mike wasn't wrong. The next picture they added to their album was on the day they were given an award for Most Mail Delivered. Next came their promotion to cafeteria workers and their award for Most Soup Served. Finally, they made it onto a scare floor as full-fledged Scream Can Wranglers. And when the company had several openings in the scare department, Mike and Sulley were hired as a scare team.

On Mike's first day, he stepped onto the scare floor, clipboard in hand, smiling. Sulley walked past him. "You coming, Coach?" he asked.

Mike looked down and saw the yellow line that he'd accidentally stepped over when he was a kid. He'd come a long way since then. "You better believe it!" he answered. He stepped over the line proudly—and this time he knew it was exactly where he belonged.